The Clock Struck One

Fergus Hume

The Clock Struck One

The present edition is a reproduction of previous publication of this classic work. Minor typographical errors may have been corrected without note; however, for an authentic reading experience the spelling, punctuation, and capitalization have been retained from the original text.

ISBN: 979-8-88942-478-9

CONTENTS

Chapter I	Diana on a Bicycle	1
Chapter II	The Strange Behaviour of Dr. Scott	10
Chapter III	To Every Man His Own Fear	16
Chapter IV	More Mysteries	21
Chapter V	Mr. Edermont's High Spirits	26
Chapter VI	What Happened in the Night	31
Chapter VII	A Nine Days' Scandal	36
Chapter VIII	The Will of Julian Edermont	42
Chapter IX	An Amazing Reward	47
Chapter X	Dr. Scott Is Still Obstinate	53
Chapter XI	Preparing the Ground	59
Chapter XII	A Terrible Accusation	65
Chapter XIII	Denial	71
Chapter XIV	What Dr. Scott Saw	77
Chapter XV	The Pearl Brooch	83
Chapter XVI	Dora Is Startled	89
Chapter XVII	A Story of the Past	95
Chapter XVIII	Pallant Makes a Statement	101
Chapter XIX	More Mysteries	106
Chapter XX	The Sins of the Father	112
Chapter XXI	So Near, and Yet So Far	118
Chapter XXII	What Dora Discovered	124
Chapter XXIII	The Madness of Lambert Joad	130
Chapter XXIV	The Stolen Manuscript	135
Chapter XXV	Confession	141
Chapter XXVI	A Final Surprise	148

CHAPTER I

DIANA ON A BICYCLE

Over the bridge which spans the railway two miles from Canterbury a girl was riding a bicycle. She was perfect mistress of her machine—and nerves; for on the slope of the hill she let the wheels run freely, and did not trouble to use the brake. The white dust clouded the air as she spun down to the level; and the heat of the day—a July noon—was so great that she was fain to dismount for the sake of coolness. A wayside fence offered a tempting seat; and, with a questioning glance to right and left, the girl balanced herself lightly on the topmost rail. Here she perched in a meditative fashion, and fanned her flushed face with her straw hat. A pretty girl in so unconventional a position, unchaperoned and fearless, would have shocked the susceptibilities of our grandmothers. But this is the age of the New Woman, and the girl was a type of her epoch.

Assuredly a finer representative could not have been found. She was tall and straight, deep-bosomed and stately. Her sunburnt complexion, her serviceable tailor-made dress and her stout shoes of brown leather, denoted a preference for life out of doors. Across her broad forehead, round her well-shaped head, fluttered tiny curls in a loose mass of burnished gold. For the rest, a nose aquiline and two steady eyes of gray, a mouth rather wide, red-lipped and firm; there you have a portrait in your mind's eye of a charming gentlewoman—new style. Diana must have been just such another; but for brightness, sympathy, and womanly kindness the maid surpassed the goddess. If mythology is to be credited, Diana was cold, serene and—vide Actæon's disaster—a trifle cruel. On the whole, this mortal was more lovable than that immortal, and less dangerous; otherwise the comparison holds good. Miss Dora Carew was a modern Diana—on a bicycle.

Shortly, Diana of Kent reassumed her hat, and, folding her arms, stared absently across the fields. She saw not sheep or meadow, hedge or ditch, windmill or rustling tree, for her mind was absorbed in her own thoughts; and these—as indexed by her changing expressions—did not seem to be over-pleasant. Dora frowned, smiled, wrinkled her forehead into two perpendicular lines between the eyebrows, and finally made a gesture of impatience; this last drawn forth by a glance at her watch.

"I do wish he would be punctual," she muttered, jumping off the fence; "if not, I must——"

Further speech was interrupted by the crisp vibration of a bell, and immediately afterwards a second bicycle, whirling down the slope, brought a young man to her feet. He was smart, lithe and handsome; also he was full of apologies for being late, and made the most reasonable excuses, hat in hand.

"But you know, Dora, a doctor's time is not his own," he concluded; "and I was detained by a new patient—an aristocratic patient, my dear"—this he said with subdued pride—"Lady Burville, a guest at Hernwood Hall."

"Lady Burville!" replied Miss Carew, starting. "Laura Burville?"

Dr. Scott looked profoundly surprised.

"I do not know that her name is Laura," he said; "and how you came to——"

"I heard it yesterday, Allen, for the first time."

"Indeed! From whom?"

"From the lips of my guardian."

"Mr. Edermont spoke of Lady Burville?" The young doctor frowned thoughtfully. "Strange! This morning Lady Burville spoke of Mr. Edermont."

"What did she say, Allen? No, wait"—with an afterthought—"why did she call you in? Is she ill?"

"Indisposed—slightly indisposed—nothing to speak of. Yesterday she was at church, and the heat was too much for her. She fainted, and so——"

He completed the sentence with a shrug.

"Oh!" said Dora, putting much expression into the ejaculation; "and yesterday my guardian also became indisposed in church."

"Really? Chillum Church?"

"Chillum Church."

They looked questioningly at one another, the same thought in the brain of each. Here was a stranger in the neighbourhood, a guest at Hernwood Hall, and she inquired for a recluse scarcely known beyond the walls of his house. Again, here was a man who had not been absent from the district for over twenty years, who dwelt in strict retirement, and he mentioned the name—the unknown Christian name—of the strange lady. This coincidence—if it could be called so—was odd in the extreme, and even these two unsuspicious young people were struck by its singularity. Dora was the first to speak, and her remark was apparently irrelevant.

"Come with me to the Red House," said she, moving towards her bicycle. "Mr. Edermont is ill."

"Consequent upon his indisposition of yesterday, I suppose," replied Scott, following. "Since you wish it, I obey; but do not forget my position in the house."

Miss Carew waited until he glided alongside, and they were both swinging easily down the road. Then she glanced at him with a smile—a trifle roguish, and wholly charming.

"What is your position in the house, Allen?"

"Is it necessary to explain, my dear? I am the son of Mr. Edermont's oldest friend. I am one of the few people he admits to see him. With his sanction, I am your most devoted lover. But"—and here the doctor became emphatic—"Mr. Edermont will not have me as a medical attendant—he will not have anyone. So my calling to see him professionally is rather—forgive me, my dearest—is rather impertinent."

"Then you must be impertinent enough to save his life," retorted Dora sharply. "He has never been really ill before, so far as I know, and there has been no occasion for a doctor at the Red House. But now"—her face assumed a serious expression—"he is not himself. He is agitated, distraught, terrified."

"H'm! Terrified? That is strange. Are you sure that his indisposition dates from service in Chillum Church?"

"It dates from the reading of the Litany," said Dora precisely. "You know, Allen, that for years my guardian has never failed to attend morning service at Chillum. You know also—for I have told you often—that at the prayers for deliverance from battle, murder, and sudden death he is accustomed to look questioningly round the congregation. He did so yesterday, as usual, and immediately afterwards he sank back half fainting in his seat. I wished him to leave the church at once, but he refused to go until the text was given out. Then he went home."

"And since then?"

"He has shut himself up in his room, and has neither eaten nor slept. He refuses to see me or speak to me. Several times I have been to his door to inquire if I could do anything, but he will not let me enter. He refuses admittance even to Mr. Joad. And all the hours he paces up and down, talking to himself."

"What does he talk about?" asked Scott curiously.

"I cannot say, as he speaks too low for me to hear. But I caught the name of Laura Burville twice. Alarmed lest he should fall seriously ill, I wrote to you yesterday, making this appointment, and waited at the bridge to explain. What do you think of it, Allen?"

Scott shrugged his shoulders.

"I can hardly say until I see Mr. Edermont. At the present moment I can be sure only of one thing—that the sight of Lady Burville upset your guardian in the church, and vice versâ."

"But why should they be upset at the sight of one another? They are strangers."

"H'm! We cannot be certain of that," replied Allen cautiously. "That he should mention her name, that she should ask about him—these facts go to prove that, whatever they may be now to one another, they were not strangers in the past."

"Then the past must be quite twenty years ago," said Dora thoughtfully, "for Mr. Edermont has not left the Red House all that time. But what did Lady Burville say when you told her about my guardian?"

"She said—nothing. A wonderfully self-possessed little woman, although she looks like a doll and talks like a fool, Dora; therefore the fact of her fainting yesterday in church is all the more strange. I said that Mr. Edermont was averse to strangers, that he dwelt in the Red House, and that he was a good friend to me."

"You did not mention my name?"

"Dora! As though I should converse about you to a stranger! No, my dear. I merely told so much about Mr. Edermont, prescribed for the lady's nerves, and informed her host and Mr. Pallant that she would be all right to-morrow."

"And who is Mr. Pallant?"

"Did I not mention his name? Oh, he is another guest of Sir Harry's. He left the message that I was to call and see Lady Burville."

"Indeed. Why did not Sir Harry call in his own doctor?"

"Faith! that is more than I can say," replied Scott. "All the better for me that he did not. But how this Mr. Pallant found me out I do not know. It is my impression that, hearing he was riding into Canterbury, Lady Burville asked him privately to send her a doctor, and as he chanced on my door-plate first, he called on me. A lucky accident for a struggling practitioner, eh, Dora?"

"No doubt—if it was an accident," said she dryly. "What is this Mr. Pallant like, Allen?"

"A red-haired, blue-eyed, supercilious beast. I disliked him at sight. Rather a shame on my part, seeing that he has done me a good turn."

By this time they had arrived at the outskirts of Chillum, and alighted before a massive gate of wood set in a high brick wall, decorated at the top with broken glass.

The green spires of poplar-trees rose over the summit of this wall, and further back could be seen the red-tiled gable of a house. Opposite the gates on the other side of the dusty white road there was a small cottage buried in a plantation of fir-trees. An untidy garden extended from its front-door to the quickset hedge which divided the grounds from the highway, and the house had a desolate and solitary look, as though rarely inhabited.

"Does old Joad still sleep in his cottage?" asked Allen, with a careless glance at the tiny house.

"Of course! You know Mr. Edermont won't let anyone stay in the house at night but myself and Meg Gance."

"That is the cook?"

"Cook, housemaid, general servant, and all the rest of it," replied Dora gaily; "she and I between us manage the domestic affairs of the mansion. Mr. Edermont is too taken up with his library and Mr. Joad to pay attention to such details."

"He is always in the clouds," assented Allen, smiling. "By the way, who is Mr. Joad?"

Dora laughed and shrugged her shoulders.

"I'm sure I can't tell you that," she replied carelessly; "he is an old college friend of my guardian's, who gives him house-room."

"But not a bed?"

"No. Joad has to turn out at nine o'clock every night and return to his cottage. I believe he passes most of his evenings in the company of Mr. Pride."

"Pride, Pride?" said Allen thoughtfully—"oh, that is the chubby little man who is so like your guardian."

"He is like him in the distance," answered Dora, "but a nearer view dispels the illusion. Pride is, as you say, chubby, while Mr. Edermont is rather lean. But they are both short, both have heads of silvery hair, and both rejoice in patriarchal beards. Yes, they are not unlike one another."

While this conversation was taking place the young people were standing patiently before the jealously-closed gate. Dora had rung the bell twice, but as yet there was no sign that they would be admitted. The sun was so hot, the road so dusty, that Allen became impatient.

"Haven't you the key of the gate yourself, Dora?"

"No. Mr. Edermont won't allow anyone to have the key but himself. I don't know why."

"Let us go round to the little postern at the side of the wall," suggested Allen.

Dora shook her head with a laugh.

"Locked, my dear, locked. Mr. Edermont keeps the postern as firmly closed as these gates."

"A most extraordinary man!" retorted Scott, raising his eyebrows. "I wonder what he can be afraid of in this eminently respectable neighbourhood."

"I think I can tell you, Allen."

"Can you, my dear? Then Mr. Edermont has said why——"

"He has said nothing," interrupted Dora, "but I have eyes and ears, my dear Allen. Mr. Edermont is afraid of losing his——"

"His money," interrupted Allen in his turn. "Oh yes, of course."

"There is no 'of course' in the matter," said Miss Carew sharply; "he is afraid of losing his life."

"His life? Dora!"

"I am sure of it, Allen. Remember his favourite prayer in the Litany—the prayer which takes his wandering eyes round the church: 'From battle and murder, and from sudden death, good Lord, deliver us.'"

CHAPTER II

THE STRANGE BEHAVIOUR OF DR. SCOTT

The appearance of the individual who admitted them into what may be called the prison of Mr. Edermont was sufficiently odd to merit a description. Lambert Joad, the friend, factotum, and parasite of Dora's guardian, was a short, stout man verging on sixty years. He had a large bland face, clean-shaven, and bluish-red in hue; his mouth was loose, his chin double, his jowl pendulous; and his insignificant nose was scarcely redeemed by two watery eyes of a pale blue. A few tufts of white hair covered sparsely the baldness of his skull; and his ears, hands, and feet were all large and ill-shaped. He dressed in rusty black, wore carpet slippers, and a wisp of white ribbon did duty as a collar. This last adornment hinted at a clerical vocation, and hinted rightly, for Lambert Joad was an unsuccessful parson of the Anglican Church.

Some forty years previously he had been a college friend of Edermont's, and in due course had taken orders, but either from lack of brains, or of eloquence, or perhaps from his Quilpish looks, he had failed to gain as much as a curacy. In lieu thereof he had earned a bare subsistence by making notes in the British Museum for various employers, and it was while thus engaged that Edermont had chanced upon him again; out of sheer pity the owner of the Red House had taken the unlucky Joad to Kent, and there permitted him to potter about library and garden—a vegetable existence which completely satisfied the unambitious brain of the creature. He was devoted to the god who had given him this ease.

But the odd part of the arrangement was that Edermont would not permit his hanger-on to remain in the house at night. Punctually at nine Mr. Joad betook himself to the small cottage fronting the gates, and there ate and slept until nine the next morning, when he presented himself again in the library, to read, and dust, and arrange, and catalogue the many books. For twenty years this contract had been faithfully carried out by the pair of college friends. From nine to nine daylight Joad haunted the house; from nine to nine darkness he remained in his tumbledown cottage.

Being now on duty, he admitted Dora and her lover, and after closing the gates, stood staring at them; with a book hugged to his breast, and a cunning look in his eyes. His swollen and red nose suggested snuff; his trembling hands and bloodshot eyes, drink; so that on the whole he was by no means a pleasant spectacle to behold. Dora threw a look of disgust on this disreputable, dirty Silenus, whom she particularly disliked, and addressed him sharply, according to custom.

"Where is Mr. Edermont?" said she, stepping back from his immediate neighbourhood; "I have brought Dr. Scott to see him."

"Julian is still in his bedroom," replied this Silenus in a voice of surprising beauty and volume; "but he does not wish to see anyone, least of all a doctor."

"Oh, never mind that, Mr. Joad," said Allen good-humouredly. "I come as a friend to inquire after the health of Mr. Edermont."

"I quite understand," grunted the other; "you will make medical suggestions in the guise of friendly remarks. So like your father, that is."

"My father, Mr. Joad? Did you know him?" asked Scott, considerably astonished.

"Yes; I do not think," added Joad, with a spice of maliciousness, "that you had that advantage."

"He died when I was five years old," replied Allen sadly, "so I remember him very slightly. But it is strange that I should have known you all these months without becoming aware of the fact that you were acquainted with my father."

"All this is beside the point," broke in Dora severely. "I want you to see Mr. Edermont. Afterwards you can talk to Mr. Joad."

"I shall be glad to do so. There are many things I wish to know about my father."

"Then, why ask me, Dr. Scott, when Julian is at hand?"

"Mr. Edermont refuses to answer my inquiries."

"In that case," said Joad, with great deliberation, "I should ask Lady Burville."

The young man was so startled by this speech that for the moment he could say nothing. By the time he had recovered his tongue Joad was already halfway across the lawn. Scott would have followed him, but that Dora laid a detaining hand upon his arm.

"Later on, Allen," she said firmly; "in the meantime, see my guardian."

"But, Dora, Lady Burville's name again hints——"

"It hints at all manner of strange things, Allen. I know that as well as you do. I tell you what, my dear: the coming of this woman is about to cause a change in our lives."

"Dora! On what grounds do you base such a supposition?"

"On the grounds that you know," she returned distinctly. "I can give you no others. But I have a belief, a premonition—call it what you will—that Lady Burville's coming is the herald of change. If you would know more, ask Mr. Edermont who she is, and why he fainted at the sight of her."

By this time they were standing on the steps of the porch, whence the wings of mellow red brick spread to right and left, facing the sunlit lawn. Square-framed windows extended along this front above and below, and an upper one of these over the porch was wide open. As Allen and Dora stood by the steps, a wild white face peered out and saw them in the sunlight. Had they looked up they would have seen Mr. Edermont, and have refrained from further conversation. But Fate so willed it that they talked on, unconscious of a listener. It was Allen who reopened the subject of his new patient, who had been referred to both by Edermont and Joad in so mysterious a way.

"After all," said Allen meditatively, "I do not see why you should have a premonition of change. That Lady Burville should know Mr. Edermont is nothing to you."

"Quite so; but that Lady Burville should know something about your late father is something to you. Did she mention anything about it this morning?"

"Not a word," he replied; "it was strange that she should not have done so."

"Not stranger than that you should have been called in to attend her."

"That was purely an accident."

"I don't think so," said Dora deliberately; "at least, not in the face of Mr. Joad's remark."

Dr. Scott looked puzzled.

"What do you make out of this Lady Burville?" he asked.

Before Dora could answer the question, a voice spoke to them from above.

"Do not talk any more of that woman," cried Mr. Edermont with a tremor in his tones. "Come upstairs, Allen; I have something for your private ear."

And then they heard the window hastily closed, as though Mr. Edermont were determined that the forthcoming conversation should be as private as possible.

"Go up at once, Allen," whispered Dora, pushing him towards the door. "You speak to my guardian, and I shall question Mr. Joad about Lady Burville. Mind, you must tell me all that Mr. Edermont says to you."

"There may not be anything to tell," said Allen doubtfully.

Dora looked at him seriously.

"I am sure that what is told will change your life and mine," she said.

"Dora! you know something?"

"Allen, I know nothing; I am going simply by my premonition."

"I am not superstitious," said Scott, and entered the house.

He was not superstitious, as he stated; yet at that moment he might well have been so, for in the mere act of ascending the stairs he was entering on a dark and tortuous path, at the end of which loomed the shadow of death.

When his gray tweeds vanished up the stairs, Dora turned her eyes in the direction of Mr. Joad. He was seated in a straw chair under a cedar-tree, and looked a blot on the loveliness of the view. All else was blue sky and stretches of emerald green, golden sunshine, and multicoloured flowers; this untidy, disreputable creature, a huddled up mass of dingy black, seemed out of place. But, for all that, Dora was glad he was within speaking distance, and alone. So to speak, he was the key to the problem which was then perplexing her—the problem of her premonition.

That a healthy, breezy young woman should possess so morbid a fancy seems unreasonable; and Dora took this view of the matter herself. She was troubled rarely by forebodings, by premonitions, or vague fears; nevertheless, there was a superstitious side to her character. Hitherto, in her tranquil and physically healthy existence, there had been no chance for the development of this particular side; but now, from various causes, it betrayed itself in a feeling of depression. Mr. Edermont's fainting and mention of Lady Burville; that lady's fainting and anxiety concerning the recluse; and finally, Mr. Joad's assertion that Lady Burville had known Allen's father—all these facts hinted that something was about to happen. Dora did not know what the something could possibly be, but she felt vaguely that it would affect the lives of herself and her lover. Therefore she was anxious to know the worst at once, and accordingly, going out to meet her troubles, she walked forward to the Silenus on the lawn.

Joad saw her coming, and looked up with what was meant to be a fascinating smile. This disreputable old creature had the passions of youth in spite of his age, and in his senile way he greatly admired the ward of his patron. His admiration took the annoying form of constantly forestalling her wishes. If Dora wanted a book, a paper, a chair, a bunch of flowers, Joad was always at hand to supply her wants. At first she accepted these attentions carelessly enough, deeming them little but the kindly pertinacities of an amiable old man; but of late she had found Joad and his attentions rather troublesome. Moreover, his obsequious demeanour, his leers, his oily courtesies, made her feel uneasy. Nevertheless, she did not dream that the old creature was in love with her beauty. So absurd an idea never entered her head. But Joad was in love, for all that, and cherished ardently his hopeless passion.

"Mr. Joad," said Dora abruptly, coming to the point at once, "who is Lady Burville?"

"Dear Miss Carew," cried the old man, ignoring the question, and rising to his feet, "pray be seated in this chair. The sun is hot, but here you will be out of the glare."

"Never mind about the glare and the chair," said Dora, making an unconscious rhyme; "I asked you a question. Who is Lady Burville?"

"Lady Burville?" repeated Joad, seeing he could no longer escape answering; "let me see. Mr. Pride said something about her. Oh yes: she is the wife of Sir John Burville, the celebrated African millionaire, and I believe she is the guest of Sir Harry Hernwood at the Hall."

"Go on," said Dora, seeing that he paused; "what else do you know?"

"Nothing. What I repeated was only Pride's gossip. I am ignorant of the lady's history. And if you come to that, Miss Dora," added Joad with a grotesque smile, "why should I not be ignorant?"

"But you hinted that Lady Burville knew Allen's father," persisted Dora, annoyed by his evasion of her question.

"Did I?" said Joad, suddenly conveying a vacant expression into his eyes. "I do not remember, Miss Dora. If I did, I was not thinking of what I was saying."

"You are wilfully deceiving me, Mr. Joad."

"Why should I, Miss Dora? If I knew anything about this lady I would tell you willingly; but it so happens that I know nothing."

"You spoke as though you knew a good deal, retorted Dora angrily.

"I spoke at random, young lady. And if you—why, what's the matter with Julian?"

It was little wonder that he asked the question, for Edermont had opened his window again, and was hanging out of it crying and gesticulating like some terrible Punch.

"Lambert! Lambert!" he shrieked. "Come and help me! He will kill me—kill me!"

Joad shuffled towards the house as quickly as his old legs could take him. He was followed by the astonished Dora, and they were about to step into the entrance-hall, when Allen Scott came flying down the stairs. He was wild-eyed, breathless, and as gray in hue as the clothes he wore.

"Allen!" cried Dora, recoiling at his mad looks, "what is the matter?"

"Don't stop me, for God's sake!" said the doctor hoarsely, and avoiding her outstretched hand, he fled hastily down the garden-path. A click of the gate, which had not been locked by Joad, and he vanished from their sight.

Dora stared at Joad; he looked back at her with a malicious grin at the flight of her lover, and overhead, at the open window, they heard the hysterical sobbing of Julian Edermont.

CHAPTER III

TO EVERY MAN HIS OWN FEAR

After a pause of astonishment at the inexplicable flight of her lover, Dora ran upstairs to the room of Mr. Edermont. It was imperative that she should learn the truth of this disturbance, and, in the absence of Dr. Scott, her guardian was the proper person to explain the matter. Had Dora glanced back at Joad, who followed closely, she might have gathered from his malignant expression that he was likely also to afford an explanation; but in her anxiety she went directly to the door of Mr. Edermont's bedroom. It was wide open, and the occupier was still sobbing by the open window.

"What is the matter?" cried Dora, hurrying forward. "Why has Allen——"

Edermont lifted up a white face wet with tears, and flung out two thin hands with a low cry of terror. Then, with a sudden anxiety in his eyes, he staggered rather than walked across the room, and closed the door sharply. Joad had already entered, and, still hugging a book, stood looking grimly at the swaying figure of his patron. With his back to the door, Edermont interrogated his ward and his friend.

"Has he gone? Is the gate closed—is it locked and barred?"

"He has gone, and the gate is safe," said Joad, for Dora was too astonished by the oddity of these questions to reply.

Edermont wiped the sweat from his forehead, nodded weakly, and finally subsided into an armchair. Here he bowed his face in his hands, and Dora caught the drift of the words which he muttered in a low voice. They were those of his favourite prayer from the Litany.

"'From battle and murder, and from sudden death, good Lord, deliver us,'" moaned the man; and then in some measure he recovered his serenity.

Seized with a sudden anger at the abject terror he had displayed, at the shameful accusation he had levelled against her lover, Dora stepped forward and faced Mr. Edermont with an indignant look.

"Now that you feel better," she said coldly, "perhaps you will afford me an explanation."

Edermont looked at her in a dazed manner. He was a little man, scarcely five feet in height, and had a noble head, which seemed out of place on so insignificant a body. With his long white locks and streaming beard, he was quite an imposing figure when seated; but when standing, the smallness of his body, of his hands and feet, detracted from the majesty of his patriarchal looks. Also, his eyes were timid and restless; the silvery beard, which swept his breast, hid a weak mouth; and, stripped of his venerable disguise, Mr. Edermont would, no doubt, have looked what he was—a puny, irresolute, and insignificant animal. As it was, he imposed on everyone—until they knew him better. Dora had long since fathomed the narrow selfishness of his nature, and she saw him for what he was, not as he appeared to the outside world. It is but fair to add that she always treated him with deference in public.

At the present moment there was no need to keep up appearances, and Dora spoke brusquely to the little man. In her heart she had as great a contempt for him as she had a disgust for Joad. They were both objectionable, she considered, and each had but one redeeming point—the noble head of Edermont, the noble voice of his friend. Beyond these, the first was more of a rabbit than, a man; the second rather a satyr than a human being. Never had Dora detested the pair more than she did at the present moment.

"I am waiting for your explanation, Mr. Edermont," she said again, as he did not reply.

"I have no explanation for you," retorted her guardian wearily; "go away, Dora, and leave me in peace."

The girl took a seat, and folded her arms.

"I don't leave this room until I know why Allen left the house," she said firmly.

"What has that to do with you?" cried Edermont in shrill anger; "our conversation was about private matters."

"It was about Lady Burville."

"What do you know of that woman?" he demanded, shrinking back.

"I know that the mere sight of her caused you to faint," said Dora slowly, "and I know also that she was acquainted with Allen's father."

"Lambert, you have betrayed me!" said Edermont in a tone of terror.

"You have betrayed yourself, Julian," was Joad's reply. "I can guess why Allen Scott left the house."

"I—I could not help myself. I was—oh, I was afraid," muttered Edermont, passing his hand over his eyes.

"You have cause to be afraid—now," retorted Joad; and with a look of contempt at the shrinking figure of his friend he turned and left the room. Dora waited until his heavy footsteps died away, then she turned again to Edermont.

"Why did Allen leave the house?" she asked with obstinate insistence.

"That is my business."

"And mine also. I have a right to know why you have driven away the man whom I am about to marry."

Edermont burst into unpleasant mirth. "That's all over and done with, my dear," he said, staring at her. "Allen Scott will never marry you—now."

"What have you told him?" she gasped, turning pale.

"I have told him something which will keep him away from this house—something which will prevent him from ever seeing you again."

"What do you mean, Mr. Edermont?"

She had risen to her feet, and was standing over him with flushed face and indignant eyes. To force his speech she gripped the shoulder of the man until he winced with pain.

"You have said something against me," she continued, giving him a slight shake.

"I have been saying nothing against you. I am truly sorry for you, Dora."

"Sorry for me, Mr. Edermont? Why?"

"Because of your parents," said her guardian slowly.

Dora stepped back. Since she had been brought by Edermont to the Red House, a year-old babe, he had never mentioned the name of her parents. All questions she had put to him had been put aside. That her father and mother were dead, that she inherited five hundred a year, and that Mr. Edermont was her guardian until she reached the age of twenty-one—these facts were known to her; beyond them, nothing. Now it would seem that some mystery was connected with the dead, and that Mr. Edermont was about to divulge it.

"What did my parents do that you should be sorry for me?" she asked pointedly.

"I shall never tell you what they did, Dora. I have hinted too much already. It is sufficient for you to know that they sinned, and that their sin will be visited on you."

"How dare you speak to me like this!" cried Dora, clenching her hands; "what right have you to terrify me with vague hints? I demand an explanation!"

"You will never obtain one—from me," said Edermont in a quavering voice; "and if you are wise you will seek one nowhere else."

"I shall ask Allen."

"He is bound by a promise to me not to tell you."

"Then, I shall question Lady Burville."

Edermont rose with a bound, and gripped her arm with a strength of which she had not thought him capable.

"Girl," he cried earnestly, "do not go near that woman! She is an evil woman—one who has brought harm in the past, and will bring harm in the future. When I saw her in church it was no wonder that I turned faint. She has hunted me down; and she brings trouble in her train. Leave me to fight my own battles, Dora, and come not into the fray. If you cross her path she will show you such mercy as she has shown me. I implore you to say nothing, to think nothing. If you disobey me I cannot save you; you must be your own salvation."

Throughout this strange speech he kept his eyes fixed upon her face. When it was ended he dropped her arm and turned away.

"Leave me now," he said faintly; "I—I am not myself."

The poor creature seemed so exhausted that it would have been absolute cruelty to have questioned him further, and, anxious as Dora was to do so, she was moved from sheer pity to spare him. Without a word she left the room, closing the door after her, and went slowly downstairs to the hall. Here she paused and considered.

"I knew that some evil was coming," she thought, with a chill of fear, "and my premonition has come to pass. According to that coward upstairs, there is danger and evil on all sides. He has separated me from Allen; he warns me against Lady Burville; yet he refuses to enlighten my ignorance, and warns me against going to others. But I must know; I must learn what it is that threatens the future happiness of Allen and myself. I can't sit down with folded arms and await the bolt from the blue. I must know, I must consider, I must act."

Against two people Edermont had warned her, but he had omitted to specify a third. Out on the lawn, under the cedars, Dora saw the black figure of Joad. It would appear from his parting words to his patron that he knew what had been told to Allen. Dora was on the point of crossing to him, and wringing, if possible, the truth from his reluctant lips, but her instinctive repulsion to the man prevented her from taking him into her confidence. If she wanted help, she must rely on herself or upon Allen. He was her affianced lover, and she felt that she could trust him. But if his lips were sealed by the promise given to Edermont, why——

"But he will tell me—he must tell me," she said, with an angry stamp. "I shall go into Canterbury at once." She glanced at the old clock in the hall, which chimed half-past two. "I shall go at once," repeated Dora, and went for her bicycle.

At the gate she found Joad, with the key in his hand. He cast a sidelong look at her bicycle, and explained his presence on the spot.

"I quite forgot to lock the gate, Miss Dora," he said, in his deep tones; "it was fortunate for Dr. Scott that I did not, and unfortunate for you."

"Why was it unfortunate for me, Mr. Joad?" she asked coldly.

"Because, if Dr. Scott had not been able to get out, he would have been forced to remain; and if he had remained," said Joad, with another glance at the machine, "he might have saved you a journey to Canterbury."

"How do you know that I am going to Canterbury?"

"I guessed it. You wish to obtain from Scott the explanation which Julian refuses. As I said, it was unlucky Scott found this gate unlocked, else he might have made his explanation here."

"You are a shrewd observer, Mr. Joad," was Dora's reply; "and I admit that you are right. I am going to see Dr. Scott, as you say."

"It is a hot day, and a long journey. You will experience discomfort."

"Probably I shall," said Dora, with a significant look. "Suppose you save me the journey, Mr. Joad, and explain this mystery yourself?"

"To what mystery are you alluding, young lady?" asked Joad with childlike blandness.

"To the mystery of Allen's sudden departure. You know the reason for it. I heard you say so myself to Edermont."

"Mr. Edermont's secrets are not my secrets, and I do not betray my friends."

"You are wonderfully scrupulous," said Miss Carew scornfully. "Well, I won't ask you to play the part of a traitor. Allen will tell me what I want to know."

"I am afraid Allen will do no such thing, Miss Dora."

"I have a right to know what bar there is to my marriage."

"I agree with you there," replied Joad, putting the key in the lock of the gate. "All the same, Dr. Scott will keep his own counsel. But I'll tell you one thing, Miss Dora—Julian is right: you will never marry Allen Scott."

"Who will stop the marriage?" asked Dora indignantly.

"Scott himself. He will ask you to break the engagement."

Dora looked at Joad with ineffable contempt, and wheeled the bicycle out on the dusty road.

"I will never believe that until I hear it from his own lips," she said. And the next moment she was spinning at full speed towards Canterbury.

Joad looked after her with a grim smile, and locked the gates with the greatest deliberation. Then he went up to the house, swinging the key on his finger and talking aloud.

"This," said Joad, chuckling, "is the beginning of the end."

CHAPTER IV

MORE MYSTERIES

If Dora was disappointed at failing to obtain explanations at Chillum, she was still more so at Canterbury. She ran the five miles under thirty minutes, and made sure she would be able to overtake Allen before he could escape her. There was a vague idea in her mind that, owing to what had been told him by Edermont—whatever it might be—he did not wish to submit himself to her questioning. This idea was confirmed by the discovery she made on reaching the tidy green-doored house near the Cathedral. Dr. Scott was not at home.

"And to tell the truth, miss," said Mrs. Tice, a large, ample, motherly person, who had been Allen's nurse and was now his housekeeper, "the doctor has gone to London."

"To London?" gasped Dora blankly, "and without letting me know?"

"Dear, dear; did he say nothing, miss? Well, to be sure! and Mr. Allen so considerate! You'll pardon me, miss, but I have been with him since he was a baby, and I should be sorry to think he had quarrelled with you. It's few as loves as Mr. Allen does."

"There is no quarrel," said Miss Carew, a trifle stiffly. "Dr. Scott saw my guardian, and then left the house without speaking to me. I have called to ask for an explanation."

"Well, miss, I'll—but, dear, dear! here I am keeping you out on the doorstep. A fine rage Mr. Allen would be in if he knew that, miss. Come in and rest, my dear lady, and I'll make you a cup of tea."

Dora accepted this hospitable offer with alacrity, not that she was anxious for rest or tea, but because it occurred to her that Mrs. Tice might throw some light on the darksome mysteries which were perplexing her brain. The old woman, as she had stated, had taken charge of Allen since he was a baby, so she, if anyone, would know about this Lady Burville who had been acquainted with Scott senior. But before Dora asked any questions concerning this remote past, she wanted first to learn the circumstances of Allen's hasty departure for London. When seated in Mrs. Tice's comfortable room, she spoke directly on the subject.

"Had Dr. Scott decided to go up to town this morning?"

"Why, no, miss," replied the housekeeper, poising a spoon over the caddy, "and that is just what puzzles me. Mr. Allen is not a young gentleman to make up his mind in a hurry like. But he came home about half an hour ago quite wild in his looks, and would not say what ailed him. Before I could turn round, he had put a few things into a black bag, and went off on his bicycle."

"To the station?"

"No, Miss: to Selling. He said he had a patient to see there, and would catch the four twenty-six train from that place."

Dora glanced at her watch. It was now three o'clock, and if she chose she could ride the nine miles to Selling before the up-train left that station. But this she determined not to do. If Allen insisted upon behaving so badly, she would do nothing to force him into an explanation. Sooner or later he would tell her his reasons for this strange conduct. But there was no doubt in her mind that his sudden departure was the result of his mysterious conversation with Mr. Edermont.

"When did Mr. Scott say he would return, Mrs. Tice?"

"To-morrow, miss; and then I have no doubt he will explain why he went off in such a hurry."

"He did not tell you, I suppose?"

"Not a word, miss," replied the housekeeper, pouring out the tea. "He'll be in a rare way when he finds out you have been here, and he not at home to make things pleasant for you. Your tea, miss."

"You will make them pleasant enough, Mrs. Tice. What delicious tea and bread and butter! I feel quite hungry after my ride. By the way," continued Dora, artfully preparing to take the housekeeper by surprise, "Allen told me that he had a new patient—Lady Burville."

Contrary to her expectation, Mrs. Tice did not appear to be astonished. From the composed expression of her face, from the friendly nod with which she received the news, Dora was convinced that she was absolutely unacquainted with the name. Failing in this attack, Dora attempted to gain the information she wanted, if it were to be gained, by approaching the subject from another quarter.

"I am so glad that the doctor is to prescribe for Lady Burville," she said softly; "she will be able to do Allen so much good in his profession. He only needs the chance, and with his talents he is sure to be successful."

"Mr. Allen is very clever indeed," said delighted Mrs. Tice, who could never hear her nursling praised sufficiently.

"And his father was clever also, I believe?" said Dora, unmasking her batteries. This time Mrs. Tice changed colour, and placed the cup she was holding carefully on the tray. Dora noticed that her hand trembled.

"The late Dr. Scott was eminent in his profession," she said in a low voice.

"What a pity he did not live to help Allen on!" pursued Dora, still observant; "how long ago is it since he died, Mrs. Tice?"

"Some twenty years, miss."

"Really! When Allen was five years old; and you have had charge of him ever since?"

Mrs. Tice recovered a little of her self-control.

"I had charge of him before that, miss," she said genially; "his poor mother died when he was born, so I have had him in my care since he was in his cradle. And, please God, I'll stay with him until I die—that is, miss, if you do not object to my continuing housekeeper after your marriage to my dear Mr. Allen?"

"You shall stay and look after us both," declared Dora impetuously; "we could not do without you."

"Your guardian, Mr. Edermont, will miss you when you marry, my dear lady."

Dora's lip curled. "I do not think so," she said quietly. "Mr. Edermont is too much wrapped up in himself to trouble about me. You have never seen him, have you?" And on receiving a shake of the head, Dora continued: "He is a little womanish man, with a fine head of silvery hair."

"Ah!" said Mrs. Tice, a startled expression coming into her eyes.

"I think he has quarrelled with Allen," pursued Dora, not noticing the change in the other's manner, "for he told him something which may prevent our marriage."

"What was it, my dear?" asked Mrs. Tice in some perturbation.

"I don't know; Mr. Edermont won't tell me. And I asked you about this Lady Burville because I feel sure she has something to do with it."

"But, Miss Carew, I do not understand!"

"Well, Mrs. Tice," cried Dora quickly, "Mr. Joad said Lady Burville knew my guardian and Allen's father, and—I'm sure I can't tell how—but it has something to do with our marriage being stopped and Allen's going to London."

By this time Mrs. Tice was perfectly livid, and trembling like a leaf. Out of the incoherencies of Dora's story she had picked an idea, and it was this which moved her so deeply. Dora looked at her in astonishment.

"What is the matter, Mrs. Tice? Are you ill?"

The housekeeper shook her head; then, rising with some difficulty, she went to a cupboard, and produced therefrom a book of portraits. Turning over the pages of this, she pointed out one to Dora.

"A little man with silvery hair," she said slowly—"is that your guardian, Miss Carew?"

Dora looked and saw the face—clean-shaven—of a young man. Notwithstanding the absence of beard, she recognised it at once. It was Julian Edermont, with some twenty years off his life.

"Yes, that is Mr. Edermont," she said, astonished at the discovery.

"And you are his—his daughter?" questioned the housekeeper.

"No; I am his ward. Mr. Edermont has never been married."

Mrs. Tice looked thoroughly frightened.

"You say Mr. Edermont had a conversation with Mr. Allen?"

"Yes: a conversation and a quarrel."

"Oh, great heavens! if he should have learnt the truth!" muttered the old lady.

"If who should have learnt the truth?" demanded Dora.

Mrs. Tice closed the book with a snap, and put it in the cupboard, shaking her head ominously. She kept her eyes turned away persistently from the face of the young girl. Whatever discovery she had made from displaying the photograph, it was evident that she did not intend to communicate it to her companion.

"How did you come possessed of Mr. Edermont's photograph, when you said you did not know him?" asked Dora suddenly.

"I did not know him until—five minutes ago. You had better ask me no more questions, Miss Carew."

"But can you not tell me, from your knowledge of Allen's parents, why Mr. Edermont has quarrelled with him?"

"If Mr. Edermont is the man I take him to be, I can. But I shall not tell you, Miss Dora."

"Why not?"

The housekeeper shuddered.

"I dare not," she said in a trembling tone. "Oh, my dear, why did you come to-day? I know much, but I dare not speak."

"Is your knowledge so very terrible?"

"It is more terrible than you can guess."

"Does Mr. Edermont know as much as you do?"

"Mr.—Edermont," said the housekeeper, with a pause before the name, "knows more than I do."

"I do not see why I should be kept in the dark," said Dora petulantly. "All that concerns Allen concerns me."

"In that case," observed Mrs. Tice calmly, "I can only recommend you to wait until Mr. Allen returns. If he chooses to tell you, well and good; but for my part, I prefer to keep silent about the past."

"But is that fair to me, Mrs. Tice?"

"Silence is more than fair to you in this case," said the old dame, looking steadily at the eager face of the young girl. "It is merciful."

"Merciful? That is a strange word to use."

"It is the only word that can be used," replied Mrs. Tice emphatically. "No, do not ask me any more, my dear young lady. The secret I hold is not my own to tell. Should Mr. Allen give me permission to reveal it, I shall do so; otherwise I prefer to be silent."

One would have thought that this speech was final; but Dora was too bent upon learning the truth of Allen's strange behaviour to be satisfied. She urged, she cajoled, she threatened, she implored, but all to no purpose. Whatever it was that Mrs. Tice knew detrimental to the past of Mr. Edermont, she was determined to keep it to herself. Evidently there was nothing left but to wait until Allen returned. From experience Dora knew that she could wheedle anything out of her easy-going lover.

"Do you know anything about Lady Burville?" asked Dora, finding she could not persuade Mrs. Tice into confessing what she knew.

"I know nothing—not even the name," said the housekeeper. "Why do you ask?"

"Because Lady Burville has something to do with the quarrel between Mr. Edermont and Allen."

"I can safely say that I know nothing on that point, Miss Carew. Lady Burville is a complete stranger to me, and, I should say, to Mr. Allen. I have never heard him speak of her."

"But Mr. Edermont knows her."

"Very probably. Mr. Edermont knows many people I am unacquainted with. You must remember, Miss Carew, that there is a vast difference between the position of a gentleman and that of a housekeeper."

"Then, Lady Burville has nothing to do with Mr. Edermont's past?"

"So far as I know she has not," replied Mrs. Tice promptly. "I don't know everything, my dear young lady."

"Can you guess the cause of this quarrel?"

"Yes. I told you so before; but I cannot speak of it."

"Do you fancy that Mr. Edermont told Allen this secret you speak of?"

Mrs. Tice made no immediate reply, but smoothed her silken apron with trembling hands. At length she said:

"I do not know. I trust he did not. But if he did speak——"

"Yes, Mrs. Tice," said Dora eagerly, "if he did speak?"

The housekeeper drew a long breath. "If he did speak," she repeated, "you will never—never—never become the wife of Allen Scott."

CHAPTER V

MR. EDERMONT'S HIGH SPIRITS

After that extraordinary conversation with Allen's housekeeper, Dora returned home more mystified than ever. Like everyone else, Mrs. Tice hinted at secrets of the past likely to affect the future, yet refused any explanation of such hints. Edermont and Joad acted in the same unsatisfactory way, and Allen, to avoid questioning, absented himself from her presence. It was all very tiresome, she thought, and perfectly inexplicable. Only one fact stood out clearly in Dora's mind, namely, that Lady Burville was responsible for all this confusion; therefore, she argued, Lady Burville must hold the clue to a possible disentanglement. This was logical.

Had Dora obeyed the impulse of her nature, she would have gone directly to the cause of these perplexities and have demanded an unravelment. She would have put her questions in the crudest form, thus:

"My guardian was moved by the sight of you, and he orders me to avoid you. Your name formed the gist of conversation between my guardian and my lover, with the result that Mr. Edermont tells me I shall never marry Allen. Mrs. Tice, who is ignorant of your inexplicable influence, asserts the same thing; and the creature Joad hints that you knew Allen's father. On the surface these matters appear to be disconnected and incoherent; but I feel certain that a word from you will render them explicable. You must say that word to me, since it is upon me that the trouble you have created has descended."

So Dora thought, ranging the facts in such vague order as her ignorance permitted; but as she did not know Lady Burville, and had no plausible excuse for seeking her, she was forced to remain in ignorance for want of the explanation which she felt sure the woman could have supplied.

In her present dilemma, Dora, with her usual good sense, recognised that there was nothing to be done but to remain quiescent, and wait. Later on Allen would return from London—indeed, Mrs. Tice expected him back that day—and then he would be forced to explain his conduct. That explanation might put the matter in a plain light, and do away with the fiats of Mrs. Tice and Edermont regarding the impossibility of her marriage with Allen. Come what might, Dora was resolved that she would not give up her lover and spoil her life. But, pending explanation and resultant adjustment of the situation, she held her peace, and waited. The future was—the future. Dora knew no more than that.

For a week after that day of mysteries, life progressed as usual at the Red House. Joad came and went with his usual punctuality, and eyed Dora in a furtive manner, with a distinct avoidance of explanation. Edermont recovered his nerve to some extent, and moved in his accustomed petty orbit; and Dora, lacking other interests, attended to her household duties. To a casual spectator, all things would seem to be going on as usual, the life would have appeared tranquil and dull; but this was but surface calm. Beneath, dangerous elements were at work, which later on were destined to—but it is no use to recur to the hackneyed simile of a sleeping volcano.

All these seven days nothing was heard of Lady Burville or of Allen. The former still continued to be a guest at Hernwood Hall, the latter still remained in London. Not a line had been received from him by Dora, and, hurt in her maidenly pride, she became offended by his continued silence. Whatever extraneous circumstances had led to his behaviour, she had not caused the breach—for breach she considered it—between them. Twice or thrice she had determined to go over to Canterbury and question Mrs. Tice, but pride withheld her. She remained at the Red House, waiting, waiting, and waiting. What else could she do?

Mention has been made of the high wall which surrounded the mansion of Mr. Edermont. This had been built by himself, and contained only two entrances, one from the road—a tall gate with spikes on the top—the other, a little door far down the right side. The house itself, like these gates, was kept always bolted and barred, and Mr. Edermont confessed to a fear of robbers. But, bearing in mind his particular prayer in the Litany, Dora was certain in her own mind that a greater fear than this moved him to take such precautions.

When Joad had retired to his cottage at nine o'clock, Mr. Edermont accompanied him personally to the gates, and saw that they were bolted and barred. Afterwards he examined the side postern, and then retreated to the mansion, where he closed the iron-clamped shutters and locked every door throughout the house. The woman who cooked and cleaned, and did all the work, was locked up in the kitchen, with bedroom adjoining, like a prisoner; Dora was barred in her own set of rooms, and Mr. Edermont shut himself up in equal isolation. Ever since Dora could remember, these precautions had been taken, and by night she felt as though she were in gaol. Certainly burglars could not break in; but, on the other hand, none of the three inmates could get out unless permitted to do so by the caprice of Mr. Edermont. And on this point he had no caprice.

A week after his conversation with Allen—the conversation which had terminated in so unexpected a manner—Edermont sat in his study. This was a small oak-panelled room on the left side of the house, and was entered directly from the hall. It was plainly, even penuriously, furnished, containing little beyond a bureau of innumerable drawers and cupboards, a dingy sofa, and three chairs, the most comfortable of which was placed in front of the desk. On the walls were paintings dark with age, and an assortment of flint pistols, ancient swords, savage weapons from Africa and the South Seas, and portions of rusty armour. A window looked out directly on the lawn, but there were two doors, one of which led into the hall, the other, on the opposite side, into the faded and lonely drawing-room, which was never used. This latter apartment had three windows in the same position as that of the study, and also a glass-door with shutters at the side of the house. The view from this door was bounded by a hedge of untrimmed laurel-trees. So much for the scene. Now for the drama.

To Edermont, seated at his desk on this particular morning, entered Joad, with a card held between a dingy finger and thumb. He advanced towards his friend with a malignant grin, and dropped the card on to the blotting-pad.

"Here is something likely to startle you, Julian," said he with his usual familiarity. "Mr. Augustus Pallant, on behalf of Laura Burville, is waiting to see you."

The miserable Edermont turned pale, and began to whimper.

"Oh, Lambert, do you think he means to do me harm?"

"If he does, it is on behalf of your dear Laura," replied Joad quietly; "you had better pluck up your courage, Julian, and see him."

"It might be dangerous, Lambert. Oh dear, terribly dangerous!"

"It will be more dangerous if you don't see the man."

"Why so? After twenty years Laura can do nothing."

"I am not so sure of that, Julian. She might tell Dora who she is."

The mere suggestion struck a blow at the timid heart of Edermont.

"I'll see him! I'll see him!" he cried, getting nervously on his feet. "Admit him, Lambert, and bring him here. But"—he buttonholed his friend—"remain within hearing, Lambert. He might do me an injury. I am not strong, you know."

"You are a contemptible little coward!" snarled Joad, shaking him off. "I'll look after you. There is too much to lose for me to risk your death."

Edermont threw up his hands with a cry.

"Not that word, Lambert; there can be no danger after twenty years. 'From battle and murder, and from sudden death, good Lord, deliver us.'"

As was his custom, Joad sneered at this prayer, which Edermont had offered up daily for the last twenty years, and went out of the house. In a few minutes he returned with a tall, red-haired man, whom he introduced silently into the study. After the introduction he closed the door, and went across to his favourite seat under the cedar to await events. The first which occurred was the coming of Dora.

She had seen the introduction of the stranger from her window, and, wondering what the visit might portend—for visitors were rare at the Red House—she waited a reasonable time, then sought Joad on the lawn. He looked up at her graceful figure with admiration in his eyes—a look which Dora resented. It had occurred to her on more than one occasion that, notwithstanding his age and physical defects, this creature, as she termed him, had presumed to fall in love with her. However, as at present he limited his mistaken passion to looks, she merely frowned at his amorous glances, and asked her question.

"Why has Mr. Pallant called?" she demanded.

"How do you know that is his name?" asked Joad, without altering his position.

"Dr. Scott described him to me," she said curtly. "Why has he called?"

"Julian can answer that question better than I can," answered Joad, with a chuckle at baffling her curiosity, and returned to his reading.

Dora, who knew that he revenged himself thus for the frown she had bestowed on him, strove to assuage his childish petulance.

"I think you might be civil, Mr. Joad," said she in an offended tone. "I have no friend but you."

"What about Allen Scott?"

"There is no question of friendship there," said Dora stiffly. "Allen Scott is my affianced husband."

"Ho, ho! Your affianced husband!" jeered Silenus, grinning. "Well, Miss Dora, while Dr. Scott holds that position, I am no friend to you."

"Why not?" asked Dora, nettled by the hinted menace in his tone.

"It's too long to explain; it's too early yet for plain speaking. But look you here, Miss Dora: a man is as old as he feels, not as he looks. I feel twenty-two—and at twenty-two"—he leant forward with a sly smile—"one falls in love."

"You are talking nonsense!" retorted Miss Carew, drawing back; "and your conversation is not to the point. I ask you why Mr. Pallant called to see my guardian."

"And I answer as I answered before," replied Joad, rendered sullen by the rebuff, "that you had better ask Julian. As I am not your friend, you can't ask me to tell you my secrets."

"I don't want to know your secrets, but those of Mr. Edermont."

"Then, speak to the right person," said Joad rudely. "I am not Julian."

After which speech he began reading again, utterly oblivious of the presence of the girl he admired. Dora made no reply, but went back to the house. At the door she was met by her guardian in a state of wild excitement. He ran out, shouting and holding out his hands. Behind him appeared the tall and well-dressed form of Mr. Pallant.

"Dora! Lambert!" shouted Edermont wildly. "Congratulate me! My nightmare is at an end! I am free! I am safe!"

Then he ran over to Joad, and talked to him with much gesticulation.

Thinking her guardian had suddenly gone out of his mind, Dora turned to Mr. Pallant for an explanation. He stared at her with undisguised admiration, and she resented it, as she had done that of Joad, with a frown.

"What is the matter with Mr. Edermont?" she asked abruptly.

"Why," said Mr. Pallant in a slow and sleepy voice, "I have brought him some good news."

"What good news?"

"I think Mr. Edermont will inform you himself," said Pallant.

And at that moment Edermont, still overwhelmed with joy, came running back.

"I am safe—safe!" he shouted; "and after twenty years of dread. No more of the Litany, no more of the—O God!"

His joy was too much for him, and he rolled over on the ground in a dead faint, at the very feet of Dora and Pallant.

CHAPTER VI

WHAT HAPPENED IN THE NIGHT

And here was another mystery: Dora never learnt the good news which Pallant had brought to Edermont. The little man had fainted with excess of joy, and was carried off to bed by Joad; while Pallant took his leave of Dora, and was escorted by her to the gate. He smiled as she turned the key of the lock.

"No need for that now," said he, passing through the gate. "Mr. Edermont can sleep in peace without bolt or bar."

"On account of what you have told him to-day?"

"Precisely, Miss Carew; on account of what I have told him to-day."

Dora looked at his sneering mouth, at his bold blue eyes, and asked a question which had been in her mind since she had seen him from the window.

"Were you sent by Lady Burville to tell this news, Mr. Pallant?"

"No; I came of my own accord. May I ask what you know of Lady Burville?"

"I know nothing," said Dora gloomily. "I wish I did."

"Why, Miss Carew?"

The girl did not reply. Pallant was a stranger to her, and she did not care to tell him of her belief that the fatal name of Lady Burville had made trouble between herself and Allen. Pallant noticed her hesitation.

"I see you do not wish to speak to me openly," he said, sneering, "yet you may be glad to do so some day. Good-day, Miss Carew, and remember my words."

His horse was tethered to the wall, and on bidding her farewell he mounted to ride off. From the saddle he looked down at her fair face and smiled. Then he made a strange remark:

"I shall give you one last warning, Miss Carew: Beware of Allen Scott!"

The girl stared after him in surprise. Was all the world in conspiracy to torture her with hints and mysteries? Joad, Edermont, Allen and Mrs. Tice all knew of something about which they refused to speak. It would seem that Pallant—a complete stranger—was possessed also of the same knowledge. What did he mean by his warning? What had he to do with Allen Scott, or even with Edermont? Dora felt as though she were spied upon by a hundred eyes; as though she were playing a mechanical part in some terrible drama, without knowing plot, or actors, or end. She was ignorant, and therefore helpless.

For the next few days she tried to learn from Joad and her guardian what all these doings meant. Both of them refused to speak, and the tension of Dora's nerves was only relaxed by a letter from Allen, in which he stated that he would return on the second of August, and would see her the next day.

"He means to explain," thought the girl, putting the welcome letter away in her desk. "In two or three days I shall know why he quarrelled with my guardian, and why Mr. Pallant warned me against him. But I must scold Allen for his neglect."

The communication relieved her greatly. Of late she had been so bewildered and harassed that she had almost doubted whether Allen loved her truly. Yet he had told her so a hundred times, and she was satisfied that he spoke truly, from that subtle instinct which never deceives a woman. He loved her, he adored her, and none other than she would ever be his wife. Before that belief the dismal prophecies of Mrs. Tice and Edermont, the strange warning of Pallant, counted as nothing. Dora believed that Allen loved her, and could explain away all the mysteries of the past weeks. In that belief she was content to wait.

And all this time Mr. Edermont was surprisingly bright. A weight appeared to have been lifted off his shoulders, and he looked ten years younger. He was scarcely past fifty, notwithstanding his white locks and hoary beard; and he began to talk of leaving his retirement and going out to mix with the world once more. Dora knew that he had a large income, and could afford to live in the most luxurious manner. It had often been a surprise to her that he had lived so long in seclusion and almost penury. From sundry circumstances she gathered that he had for years been labouring under a dread of death by violence, hence his anxiety that the house should be carefully locked up. Now that dread had been removed—as he more than hinted—by a communication from Pallant, and he could take life easily. Looking back on the fears which had haunted him these twenty years, Dora no longer wondered at the cowardice and terror of the puny creature. Rather was she astonished that with so terrific a shadow to fight he had kept himself out of a lunatic asylum. Stronger men than he succumbed to such influences.

From force of habit Edermont still locked up the house at night; he still sent Joad to the cottage over the road; but he no longer trembled at that tremendous prayer of the Litany, nor did he look round the church searching for a possible danger. Whatever the mystery of his life could be—and Dora was quite unable to guess it—

that mystery had been done away with, and Edermont talked of fraternizing again with his fellow-creatures.

One thing struck her as odd. When he recovered from the excess of joy caused by the communication of Pallant, he wrote a lengthy letter, and this he was particular to post himself. As a rule, Joad attended to the despatch of such rare epistles as were sent from the Red House, so Dora was astonished that her guardian should be so anxious about this especial letter. It occurred to her that it might possibly have been sent to Lady Burville, with whom she felt certain her guardian was connected in some underhanded way. But she had never learnt if her belief were correct. What she did learn, however, was that Edermont wrote to Allen at Canterbury during the last days of July; also, he sent a third letter, but to whom Dora did not know. The first and last of these communications were posted with his own hand; the middle one had been delivered to Joad in the usual way.

On the night of the second of August, Edermont dismissed Joad as usual, and locked the gates according to custom. Then he returned to bolt and bar the house. In his study he found Dora awaiting him.

"You have not seen to the little postern," she said.

"No matter," he replied impatiently. "I suppose it is locked; if not—why, I can afford to leave it as it is and sleep in peace. There is no more danger for me now."

"Of what danger are you talking, Mr. Edermont?"

"What is that to you?" he retorted with weak defiance. "Why are you here? Go to bed and leave my business alone!"

"I will go to bed when you have answered me one question."

"Only one?" he scoffed. "You are more moderate than most women. Well?"

"Why have you written to Allen Scott?"

"Who told you I had done so?"

"Mr. Joad."

"He is too meddlesome!" cried Edermont angrily. "If he does not take care I shall dismiss him! What right had he to show you that letter?"

"Because he knows that I am engaged to Allen."

"I tell you the engagement must be broken off."

"Why, Mr. Edermont?" asked Dora indignantly.

"Allen will tell you. I wrote to him to call and see me. When he comes you shall speak to him in my presence, and from his own lips you shall hear that he can never be your husband."

"Until then I decline to consider the engagement as broken," said Dora, very pale, but firm. "I am not going to be your dupe, Mr. Edermont. I shall force you to explain."

"I—I forbid you to—to speak to me like this!" cried Edermont, shrinking back.

"I shall speak as I choose—I am tired of your selfish tyranny; and if Allen does not make me his wife, I shall go out into the world to earn my own living. At least I have enough to live on."

"Enough to live on?" he replied slowly. "Perhaps yes, perhaps no."

"What do you mean, sir?" she demanded imperiously.

A crafty smile played over the face of Mr. Edermont, and he shrugged his shoulders.

"Wait till Allen comes: then you may learn more than you care to listen to. Now go to bed. By the way, what about your toothache?"

"Toothache?"

"Joad said something about it," was Edermont's impatient remark; "you told him that toothache kept you awake at night."

"Very true. My nights have been sleepless for the last few weeks. I have heard that dreary sounding chime in the hall clock ring from midnight till dawn. But my tooth is better to-night, thank you. I have no pain, so there is every hope that I shall have a good night's rest."

"I am glad of that, my dear," said Edermont in a softer tone than was usual with him. "I would be fond of you, Dora, if you would let me. Remember, all these years I have stood in the place of a father to you."

"I do not forget that, Mr. Edermont," answered Dora kindly; "you have been goodness itself. The parents I have lost could not have been kinder to me."

"Perhaps not so kind," said Edermont, sitting on the chair in front of his desk. "I need not talk to you about your parents, Dora."

"Why not, Mr. Edermont? I should like to know——"

"A great many things," interrupted the old man gloomily; "but for reasons of my own, which you may learn some day, I am not prepared to gratify your curiosity; and after all," he added in a significant tone, "it would do you no good to hear the story."

"It would do me this much good," said Dora spiritedly: "I should learn the obstacle which is a bar to my marriage with Allen."

"What would be the use of your knowing the obstacle, Dora? You will never get rid of it—take my word for that. Now good-night."

"Good-night," replied Dora, thinking it useless to argue further.

"I think you might kiss me before you go," grumbled Edermont. "I stand in the place of your father."

Without a word, Dora returned and touched the forehead of the old man with her fresh young lips. As she passed through the door, a glance back showed her a picture which never left her memory in afterlife. Edermont, his noble head with its white hair leaning on his hand, sat by the bureau in gloomy thought. A single candle served rather to show than to dispel the darkness; and in the gulf of pale glimmer hollowed out of the gloom the man looked like some famous portrait by an old master. The burden of years was visible in his silvery hair and sweeping beard of snow; the burden of sorrow marked itself in the hollow eyes, the wrinkled cheek and forehead, the wasted hands. He looked the incarnation of eld as seen in that spectral light, in that tenebrous atmosphere. Dora never forgot that sight.

Once in her room, she lost no time in getting to bed. Her sleepless nights of the past week had worn her out; and now that the pain had left her tooth, she was glad to take advantage of the respite. At first she thought about her guardian and his untold miseries; afterwards of Allen's strange behaviour; lastly, her thoughts wandered to Joad's sly looks and hinted terrors, until sleep rolled like a wave over her weary brain, and she became oblivious of the material world. Nature revenged herself for many vigils, and soothed her into sound slumber.

How long she had been asleep she did not know, but suddenly, for some inexplicable reason, she woke with a start, and sat up in the bed, her nerves strung to their utmost tension, faculties all on the alert. It seemed to her that she had heard a muffled cry for help, a wild appeal for mercy; but now that she was listening with all her will, she could hear nothing. All was dark and quiet: not a sound broke the silence of the still night. After a moment or two, Dora believed that she had mistaken a dream for a reality, and, laughing softly at her own folly, lay down again to sleep. As her head touched the pillow, the deep bell of the hall clock chimed "one." Remembering how often she had heard those dreary tones in the past week, Dora smiled drowsily to herself, and was soon fast asleep again. When she again woke it was dawn.

Someone was knocking furiously at the door of the bedroom. Dora leaped out of her bed, unlocked it, and flung it wide open. Meg Gance, the cook, stood shaking on the threshold, as pale as a ghost.

"Miss Dora! O Lord, miss!" gasped the terrified woman. "The master is—is—is dead!"

"Dead?" replied Dora in a dazed tone.

"Murdered! And his head! O Lord! 'tis bashed in like a pumpkin!"

CHAPTER VII

A NINE DAYS' SCANDAL

And this was the end of Julian Edermont's high spirits. For twenty years he had dreaded and guarded himself against a violent death; but the moment that the fear had been removed the end came. There was something ironical in the way in which Fate had lulled his suspicions only to smite the surer. One day he had been rejoicing in the thought that the reign of terror was over; the next he lay dead under his own roof-tree, and none knew who had slain him.

They found the body in the study, lying near the desk, which was broken open and terribly damaged. As Meg, the cook, stated, his head was smashed in like a pumpkin, and near by lay the weapon with which the deed had been done—a Zulu knobkerrie, which had been torn from the decorative weapons of the wall. Dora was an exceptionally brave woman, cool in danger and collected in trouble; but even she felt qualmish to see that revered head all beaten, all splashed with gore. The place was like a shambles. Amid the blood lay a pistol, near to the hand of the dead man, and many papers were scattered about it, tossed in confusion from the bureau.

Mr. Edermont had been nothing more to Dora than her legal guardian. He had been a selfish, cowardly creature, who had done nothing to win her love; yet, as Dora looked at the body lying there, red with blood, battered, and beaten, and bruised, she felt at once sorry and angered. The first, that so harmless—so far as she knew—a creature had been so cruelly done to death; the second, that his assassin had escaped. However, as the deed was done, and the man was dead, no time was to be lost in raising the alarm. It was just possible that the murderer might be secured if prompt measures were taken.

Dora knew now that the cry she had heard in the night had been no fancy, no dreaming, but a terrible reality; and the striking of the clock immediately afterwards enabled her to fix the exact time when the crime had been committed. However, she was wise enough to say nothing on the point until called upon to do so. But raising, with the aid of Meg, the dead body on to the sofa, she sent the woman across the road to summon Joad. Hardly had she issued the order when the voice of that very person, in surprised tones, was heard in the drawing-room off the study.

Considerably astonished at his early arrival, for it was not yet eight o'clock, Dora ran into the next room. At the door she paused in sheer amazement. The glass door at the side of the apartment had no shutters up, and was wide open, while Joad was looking through it, apparently as much taken aback by her appearance as she was by his.

"What is it? What is it?" he demanded hastily. "This door ajar—the postern gate open—you here——"

"The postern gate open?" cried Dora suddenly. "The assassin must have escaped that way."

"Assassin! What do you mean?" stammered the new-comer, turning pale with fright.

"Come in at once, Mr. Joad, and I will show you. The sight requires no explanation."

Still amazed, Joad heaved his fat body through the door, and followed Dora into the room of death. When he saw what had taken place—the blood on the floor, the dead body on the sofa—his jaw dropped, his skin turned the colour of a dirty yellow, and he stared dumbfounded at the sight. So long did he remain in his semi-trance, that Dora was obliged to shake him by the elbow to bespeak his attention.

"You see Mr. Edermont has been murdered. Meg found him like that when she came to clean up the study."

"Aye, I did for sure!" cried Meg, her coarse face blanched with dread. "Master did not lock kitchen last night, and I found doors all wide. I came here with broom and dust-pan, and there I saw he with poor head bashed to jelly."

Joad approached the sofa and examined the body, then reverently spread his handkerchief over the disfigured face.

"My poor friend!" he muttered with emotion. "And you thought that you were safe!"

"Does that mean you know who killed him?" asked Dora, making a step forward.

"No, I do not know who killed him. Julian was always afraid that he would be murdered by a certain person; but who that person is, or why he should desire Julian's death, I know no more than you do."

Dora only believed half of this statement. From what she had seen it would appear that Joad had been completely in the confidence of the dead man, and his denial seemed to be unnecessary. However, she made no comment on the speech, but with sudden suspicion asked Joad how it was he had come to the Red House before his usual time. He guessed what was in her mind, and laughed slyly.

"If you think I know anything of this terrible deed, you are wrong," said he slowly; "it is not likely I should kill the only friend I have in the world, and reduce myself to beggary."

"Good heavens, Mr. Joad! I never accused you of such a thing!" cried Dora indignantly.

"Nevertheless, you thought it, Miss Carew," he replied smoothly, "and you deemed that I had come thus early to look at my handiwork. You are wrong: it's my custom to take a short walk to get an appetite for breakfast. In crossing the fields, I saw to my amazement that the postern door was open. Knowing that Julian was particular to keep it locked, I went to see what was the matter. I came up to the house, and saw the side door was open also. In my surprise I uttered an ejaculation, and you appeared. You know the rest."

Dora did know the rest, but she did not know who had killed her guardian. However, now that a man was on the spot, she wished him to take the management of the matter into his own hands. But Joad declined to saddle himself with any such responsibility. He said that Dora was a New Woman, who thought that the weaker sex was the stronger of the two. This being the case, Mr. Joad suggested that she should prove her boast by assuming the position of the necessary male. Dora was annoyed at his niggling arguments, and disgusted at his laziness; but, not deeming the matter worth discussing, she took all authority into her own hands.

They proved to be very capable hands. She sent a man to Canterbury for the police, and put them in charge of the body and the house. To the inspector she related all she knew, and Meg followed suit. As for Joad, he interviewed the authorities on his own account, and gave the same unvarnished statement as he had given to the two women. Mr. Inspector heard all that was to be heard, saw all that was to be seen; and after leaving a couple of policemen in charge, he returned to Canterbury to rack his brains as to the whereabouts of the assassin. He also detailed a doctor to examine the body; and with this doctor came Allen.

The young man appeared haggard and ill. His face was pale, his eyes were wild, and he looked as though he had been sitting up for several nights in succession. When he saw Dora he made no effort to embrace or kiss her, but stood before her with downcast eyes, like a detected criminal. The girl was profoundly astonished at this conduct. Ordinarily Scott was blithe and light-hearted, with a smile and a word for everybody. Now he looked dejected and worried, and had not a word to say, even to the girl to whom he was betrothed. After a time Dora, finding him so unsatisfactory, took him to her own sitting-room, and sat him in a chair. Then she spoke bluntly, and with some anger, which was surely natural.

"I am glad to see you, Allen," she said abruptly, "as I wish to have an explanation of your singular conduct."

"I have none to give you," he said, flushing.

"Indeed! Then why did you come over to-day?"

"I heard of this murder, for one thing," said Allen slowly; "and for another, I wish to put an end to our engagement."

Dora started. She remembered the prophecy of Mrs. Tice and of the dead man. It had come true sooner than she expected, and in a fashion she did not anticipate. Many things might have arisen to prevent their marriage, but if she and Allen were true to one another, she hoped to overleap all obstacles. But here was the man himself—the man who had vowed a thousand times that he could not live without her—and he proposed to part. She could hardly believe her ears; and from outraged pride tears sprang to her eyes.

"I thought you loved me, Allen!" said she, then flung herself on the sofa and sobbed as though her heart would break.

Dr. Scott rose suddenly, and stood looking down at her, his face working with passion. He would fain have taken her in his arms; he would have assured her of his love and undying fidelity. But between him and Dora a shadow was standing—the shadow of a dead man.

"I do love you, Dora," said Allen, as soon as he could command his voice; "I shall always love you; but I can never make you my wife."

"But why? What is your reason?"

"I dare not tell you my reason; but you shall learn this much: Mr. Edermont told me something which parts us for ever."

"What did he tell you?"

"I dare not say."

Dora rose slowly and looked steadily into his face. His eyes dropped before hers, and he would have turned away, but she compelled him to face her.

"Allen, you know who killed Mr. Edermont."

"No, no! As God is in heaven I do not!" he said vehemently. "I have my suspicions, but they count as nothing. Don't ask me anything, Dora, for I can tell you nothing."

"At least tell me why you wish our engagement ended," said she, very pale.

"I cannot," he groaned, and sank into a chair.

"Then listen to me, Allen," she said in a firm voice. "Until you tell me the reason of this conduct I refuse to release you from the engagement. I love you; you say that you love me; so there is no reason why we should part. If you will not speak, others will; and I shall devote myself to finding out the truth. When I do find it," she added slowly, "then we may part. Until then"—her voice rose—"you are my affianced husband."

Allen rose from his chair and walked slowly towards the window, where he stood looking out at the green lawn, the brilliant sunshine. In his then mood of self-torture and sorrow, the brightness of the day seemed a cruel contrast to his own dark thoughts. His life was over, his joys were at an end; a deadly trouble, greater than he could bear, had come upon him. Yet the flowers bloomed, the birds sang, the sunlight bathed stretches of green grass and clumps of stately trees in its golden rays, as in mockery of his puny grief and trivial ruin. The contrast struck him as so ironical that he burst into bitter laughter; but the mirth thus wrung from his breaking heart ended in a sigh of regret.

"Why do you laugh, Allen?" asked Dora, scared by this cruel merriment. "Why do you not answer?"

"I laugh because of the contrast between the joy of Nature and our own sorrows," he replied, turning his pale face towards her, "and I did not reply because I was thinking."

"You heard what I said?"

He took her hands within his own, and looked at her anguished face with a great love in his eyes.

"I heard you, and I agree," said he softly. "God bless you for a good woman, Dora, for you have behaved nobly. Many a woman would have cast me off in scorn for my refusal to speak. But you are content to wait in hope. Alas, my darling!" he cried, with a burst of sorrow; "there is no hope; there never can be hope. You and I are parted as surely as though the one were following the other to the graveyard."

"But, Allen, we have committed no sin. Why should we part?"

"Because of the sins of others. Our trouble comes from the past, Dora, and it was that dead man who revealed it to me. Did I tell you what he said, you would agree with me that the only thing left to us is to kiss and part. But I dare not tell you; in mercy to yourself I spare you the burden of the secret which has made my life so bitter."

"I know that you act in all kindness, Allen, but you are wrong. It would be better to tell me all, and let me share your troubles. I am strong; I can bear anything."

"Not this, not this," replied Allen, releasing her hands and going to the door; "it would wreck your life, your happiness, as it has wrecked mine."

"Happiness!" she said in a tone of despair; "I have done with that."

"I hope not. Oh, my dear, I trust not. Time may bring you the content that I cannot give you. I accept your noble offer, Dora. Let us still continue our engagement, although we must rarely meet. But if you are wise, you will not seek to know the secret. It will bring you no good, only evil. For your own sake I keep silent. I can do no more; I can do no less."

He paused at the door, looking at her sadly. She stood in the centre of the room, a quiet and sorrowful figure in her black dress. Allen returned, and kissed her twice on the forehead; then he left her under the same roof as the dead man, and passed out of her life—as he thought—for ever.

CHAPTER VIII

THE WILL OF JULIAN EDERMONT

After that interview Allen came no more to the Red House. He was aware that his behaviour appeared shameful; for no other word was applicable to the conduct of a man who forsook a girl to whom he had been engaged a year, and refused to disclose the reason of such desertion. Yet he could act in no other way, for the bar to the marriage, as revealed by Edermont, was so insuperable and terrible that Allen could not bring himself to enlighten Dora on the subject. If things looked black against him, he would have to put up with the situation as best he could. But to justify his conduct by telling the truth—he could not do so. In mercy to herself he spared her that revelation.

But if Allen remained absent, others did not. When the fact of the murder became known, quite a stream of morbid people set forth to view the scene of the crime. Thanks to the presence of the police, and the stubborn fact of the high wall, these folk were unable to push themselves into the house; but they gathered in crowds on the road, staring and staring, as though they hoped to see through the bricks and mortar and behold the dead body within. Much speculation was rife as to the cause of the crime, but the generally accepted opinion was that Edermont had been murdered by a burglar or burglars. Indeed, Inspector Jedd inclined to this opinion himself.

This official was a fussy, pompous man, with an immense idea of his own importance; now that an opportunity occurred of displaying that importance he made the most of it. What with examining the grounds, the house, the postern-gate; what with questioning the living inmates and the doctor who had examined the body, he was as active as a squirrel, and about as useful. In his sublime self-conceit he could not see an inch beyond his nose, and accepted the first idea that came into his head. The bureau was smashed, the drawers pulled out and emptied of their contents. On these grounds Inspector Jedd concluded that the death was due to the wrath of an interrupted housebreaker.

"Tramp, you see," he said in his jerky way to admiring subordinates. "Mr. Edermont—rich house, full of treasures and loose cash—mistaken whim, very; but tramp, hearing such tales in beer-shops, believes them. He climbs over the wall; Mr. Edermont has omitted to lock side-door. Tramp enters easily—sees bureau—thinks money there. Smashes desk with the bludgeon taken from the wall"—so the inspector denominated the "knobkerrie"—"Mr. Edermont hears noise—comes in—tramp startled—turns at bay—kills Mr. Edermont. Takes what he can—steals keys from dead man and unlocks postern-gate—gets away. There you are! What could be simpler?"

None of Inspector Jedd's underlings disputed the theory of their chief, for the simple reason that they believed in it, as they would have believed in any other he chose to put forward. Joad sneered when this explanation was repeated in his hearing, but, on the plea that he knew nothing about such matters, he made no comment upon it. Dora also disagreed with Jedd, but, being a judicious young woman, she said nothing. She herself believed that the death was due to revenge, but as yet she was too uncertain of her ground, too ignorant of Mr. Edermont's past life, to venture an opinion. The reading of the dead man's will proved that her insight into the matter was keener than Jedd's.

But before the reading of the will came the holding of the inquest. Jedd gathered together all the obtainable evidence, called all the available witnesses, with the result that nothing was discovered likely to lead to the assassin's detection. The inquest was held in the dining-room of the Red House, and everybody who could obtain admittance was present; but when Dora looked round the crowded room she noted that three persons whom she expected to see were absent. These were Allen Scott, because he was her lover, and should have been at hand to support her in this trial; Mr. Pallant, as he had evidently some knowledge of Mr. Edermont's past life, and might be curious concerning his violent death; and Lady Burville, because the sight of her in church had been, as Dora truly believed, the genesis of all these woes. But none of the three put in an appearance, and their absence gave Dora food for reflection.

The first witness called was Meg Gance, the cook, who deposed that she was usually locked up in her kitchen, with bedroom attached, by the deceased. On the night of the second of August he had omitted to lock her up as usual—why, she did not know. It was her custom to rise at seven and wait till Mr. Edermont came to let her into the main portion of the house, so that she could go about her work. She was general servant as well as cook. On the morning of the third she rose as usual, but Mr. Edermont never came. To her surprise she found the door leading to the front of the house was unlocked. She passed through with broom and dust-pan to seek the study, which she usually cleaned the first thing in the morning. There she saw Mr. Edermont lying dead near the desk, with his head smashed. The bureau was smashed also, the drawers were pulled out, and their contents untidily tumbled on the floor. Near the dead body lay a pistol and a stick (the knobkerrie) which had been taken from the wall. At once she called Miss Carew. The witness stated that she had heard no noise during the night. She had noticed no tramps or suspicious characters looking round the house of late.

The second witness was Dora Carew, who stated that she had retired as usual on the previous night at half-past nine, leaving Mr. Edermont to lock up. Her guardian usually locked the door which closed the passage on the first-floor leading to her bedroom. On this night he did not do so, although she was not aware of the fact until summoned by Meg the next morning. During the night she was awakened by a cry—as it seemed to her, an appeal for mercy. She listened, but could hear nothing further, and, thinking she had been dreaming, she had lain down and gone to sleep again. When she awoke in the morning she was called by Meg to see the dead body. She was aware that Mr. Edermont considered himself a threatened man, but she had no knowledge of the person or persons whom he feared. In reply to a question, this witness stated that she heard the cry immediately before the clock in the hall struck "one." She believed that the murder had been committed at that time.

The third witness was Lambert Joad, who gave his evidence as follows:

He was accustomed to leave the Red House at nine o'clock every night for his cottage, which was on the other side of the road. On the night of the murder he left as usual, and heard the gate locked behind him. He went to his cottage, and took his supper and read. Later on he was joined by Mr. Pride, a tutor in a local private school, who was, like himself, a classical scholar. Pride talked with him till after two o'clock in the morning, when he went away. The witness was up at seven to take a walk before breakfast, as was his custom. In crossing the fields he noticed that the postern door was open. Astonished at this, and knowing that Mr. Edermont was particular about keeping the door closed, he went across to see what was the matter. On entering through the postern gate he went to the house. To gain the front-door he had to follow the path between laurel hedges, which passed by the glass door of the disused drawing-room, off the study. He saw that this door had no shutters up on the glass, as was customary, and was standing wide open. He uttered an exclamation of surprise, which brought Miss Carew into the drawing-room. She called him in, and he saw the dead body and the smashed desk. He was not aware that Mr. Edermont had enemies. The witness believed that Edermont's fancy of being threatened with a violent death was monomania. He recognised the revolver as the property of the deceased.

The fourth witness was Dr. Chambers, of Canterbury, who deposed that he had been summoned by Inspector Jedd to examine the body of the deceased. The head was smashed in by a violent blow on the left temple, and death must have been instantaneous, After giving some technical evidence relative to the injuries inflicted, this witness concluded by stating that, from the condition of the body, he was satisfied the crime had been committed between twelve and one o'clock in the morning. This assertion bore out the statement of Miss Carew, that she had heard the hall clock strike one shortly after the cry for mercy had awakened her.

The fifth and last witness was Inspector Jedd. He deposed to the state of the body, the state of the bureau, and the finding of the knobkerrie and pistol. Evidently the criminal had entered the house through the side-door of the drawing-room, which was wide open, and had retreated the same way. No clue had been obtained likely to lead to the detection of the assassin. The postern gate, usually kept locked, had been found open on the morning after the crime. Several tramps had been arrested on suspicion, but one and all had explained their movements on the night of the second. No one but deceased knew what was in the bureau, therefore witness was unable to say if anything was missing.

These five witnesses having given their evidence, the coroner summed up, after which the jury brought in a verdict that Julian Edermont had been murdered by some person or persons unknown. It was the only conclusion to which they could come in the face of such scanty facts as had been placed before them, and all present departed with the unsatisfactory feeling that the death of Mr. Edermont was a mystery, and, what is more, was likely to remain a mystery. And so a very trying and exciting day came to a conclusion.

Mr. Edermont was duly buried in Chillum churchyard, and again Dora noticed that Allen was not present at the funeral. When she returned to the house, Mr. Carver, the long, lean lawyer from Canterbury, produced the will of the dead man, and read it to herself and Joad. As Mr. Edermont had no relations, these two were the only people likely to be interested in the disposition of his property. The will was a peculiar one, and reflected the lifelong fear of Edermont. Since he had been relieved of that fear by the visit of Mr. Pallant, he had not troubled to execute another testament; so the document read by Mr. Carver showed how vivid had been his presentiment of meeting with a violent end. The result had justified his fears.

The property included the Red House and its surrounding

acres, the pictures and silver, and also the rental of three farms, amounting to two hundred a year. All this—house, pictures, silver, and income—was left to Dora, on condition that she remained at the Red House, and permitted Lambert Joad to continue his life there on the same footing as during the life of the deceased. The rest of the property, consisting of stocks and shares and various investments, amounted in all to some fifty thousand pounds. And now came the surprising part of the will. This large sum of money was left unconditionally to such person or persons as should discover and punish the assassin of the testator.

"For years," said the maker of the will, "I have been threatened with violent death by a certain enemy. Sooner or later, in spite of all my precautions, he will succeed in carrying out his wicked purpose. In that event I am content to reward the person who punishes him, or whomsoever he employs, with the sum of fifty thousand pounds. The story of my life, which sets forth how I incurred the wrath of this enemy, will be found in my bureau, sealed with my seal. Let my ward, Dora Carew, read the document, and discover the assassin, so that she can at once revenge my death and inherit my money. But in any case she is provided for, as is Lambert Joad; and the bulk of my estate must go to him or her who punishes my enemy."

Then followed the usual clauses ending the will, the signatures of the testator, and of two witnesses.

When Carver had finished there was a dead silence, which was broken by the lawyer himself.

"It is a strange will," said he, taking off his spectacles, "and hardly worded in a legal manner. But it holds good, nevertheless, so I can only recommend you, Miss Carew, or you, Mr. Joad, to gain fifty thousand pounds if you can."

"Will that sum actually be paid over to the discoverer of the assassin?" cried Joad, with sparkling eyes.

"My dear sir," said Carver, with a solemn smile on his lean face, "the man or woman who discovers the murderer of my late client will receive"—he smacked his lips—"fifty thousand pounds!"

CHAPTER IX

AN AMAZING REWARD

The extraordinary will of Julian Edermont caused a no less extraordinary sensation. Pursuant to the instructions of his late client, Carver caused the contents of the will to be published in almost every newspaper of the three kingdoms, and the advertisement was copied and printed and talked about all over the civilized world. Many of the leading London dailies devoted a leading article to discussing the eccentricity of the bequest. Of these lucubrations none was more noteworthy than that of the Morning Planet.

"Here is a chance for our amateur and professional detectives," it said. "A riddle to stimulate the curiosity; a magnificent reward to repay the solution of the same. Mr. Edermont, a recluse, dwelling in the Red House, near Canterbury, has been barbarously murdered, and fifty thousand pounds are now offered for the discovery and apprehension of his murderer. It seems that the dead man had a past, and that that past had engendered an enemy. For twenty years Mr. Edermont lived in strict retirement, and took extraordinary precautions to ensure his safety. But all in vain. The man or woman—for no one is aware of the sex of the assassin—discovered the victim, and carried out the revenge in a peculiarly brutal fashion. There is nothing to show how the assassin came or went; but the time of the committal of the crime has been ascertained by the evidence of Miss Carew, the ward of the deceased. She fancied she heard a cry, and immediately afterwards the hall clock struck one. There can be no doubt that Miss Carew really did hear a cry, and was not dreaming, as she fancied, and that such cry was the last appeal of the poor victim for mercy.

"In the will of Mr. Edermont, he mentions that the story of his life is set forth in a manuscript locked up in his bureau. It is evident that the assassin knew of the existence of this narrative, for, immediately after committing the crime, he—we will assume by way of argument that the criminal is a man—rifled the desk, and made off with the paper containing an account of his motive for revenge. He knew that such paper would condemn him, and that with its aid the officers of the law would have little difficulty in putting a rope round his neck. Doubtless such story gave his name—possibly his address—and he was aware that it thus jeopardized his safety. But be this as it may, one fact remains: that the assassin has stolen the sole clue to his discovery, and it would seem that the death of Julian Edermont must remain wrapped in mystery.

"But fifty thousand pounds! Will anyone permit this death to go unavenged when he can gain such a reward? A fortune for life, and the consciousness of having done his duty to the dead man and to society. No doubt our inglorious Vidocques, our amateur Sherlock Holmes, will set to work to unravel the mystery and gain the reward. The Red House, near Canterbury, will become the shrine of pilgrim detectives from all parts of the world. Nevertheless, in spite of their astuteness, in spite of their greed, we doubt whether the mystery will ever be solved. The sole clue, so far as we can see, is to be found in the past life of the dead man. The tale of that past life is set forth in a certain paper; such paper is in the possession of the assassin, who is himself unknown. To find the paper, they must find the assassin; without the paper the assassin cannot be found; and so matters are at a deadlock. We shall await the development of this extraordinary case with interest; but we doubt whether the fifty thousand pounds will ever be claimed. Julian Edermont is dead and buried; his assassin has escaped with the story of the motive for the crime in his pocket. Here the case stands. What light can be thrown on this darkness? What clue can be found to the cunning murderer? We wait the answer from the possible man or woman who can honestly claim fifty thousand pounds."

While the papers talked thus, while people wondered, and would-be winners of the reward set their wits to work on the facts of the case, Dora remained at the Red House. No change was made in her life, or in that of Joad. In conjunction with Meg, the girl still looked after the domestic details of the mansion; and Joad still came and went from nine to nine. He became morose after the death of his friend, and hardly addressed a word to Dora. But she was aware that he constantly watched her in a furtive manner, which in the end became exceedingly annoying. Had the terms of the will been less clear, she would have left the Red House, or have induced Joad to confine his life to his own cottage. But in order to exist, and draw her poor rental of two hundred a year, she was forced to live in the house, with Joad, dirty, disreputable and crabbed, at her elbow. She disliked the man exceedingly, the more so as she had a suspicion that he admired her; but, fettered as she was by the terms of the will, she could do nothing.

Nevertheless, she became aware, as the days went by, that she would have to make some change in her life. It was impossible that she should go on living with an illiterate servant and an admiring satyr. It was equally impossible that she could continue to remain at variance with Allen after the last interview. He neither came near her nor wrote a line to comfort her; and, angered as she was at his heartless and inexplicable conduct, she made up her mind to see him. In one way or the other she would bring the matter to an end, and treat him either as a stranger or as her affianced lover.

Again, she wished to see Carver as to her financial position. By the will she had been left certain moneys and the Red House; but she also, as she understood, possessed an income of five hundred pounds, which came to her from her parents, and once or twice Mr. Edermont had informed her that she was entitled to so much; but he stated also that he was saving it up for her against the time she came of age.

As Dora was now twenty-one, she expected that the accumulations would be considerable. Making allowance for the amounts given to her at various times, she concluded that she was entitled to close on eight thousand pounds. If this were so—as she could ascertain from Mr. Carver—it was her intention to change her mode of life should Allen prove obstinate.

"I shall give up the Red House and the two hundred a-year," thought Dora, making her plans, "and, after investing my eight thousand pounds with the aid of Mr. Carver, I shall go to London. I cannot live any longer in the company of that odious creature"—for so she termed the learned Joad. "And if Allen is resolved to break off the engagement, there is nothing to keep me here. Mr. Edermont is dead; Allen, for some reason, is estranged, and I am all alone. I shall take my life in my own hands, and go to London."

It never entered her head to earn the reward. She was completely ignorant as to how her late guardian had come to so untimely an end. Lady Burville might have explained, but after the crime she had gone to London, and Dora did not know where to find her. Mr. Pallant might have given a hint, but he had left Hernwood Hall also. Dora saw no way of solving the mystery; and even if she did conjecture the truth, she scarcely felt herself called upon to revenge the death of Mr. Edermont by discovering his assassin. She did not want the reward, and she had not sufficient regard for the dead man's memory to devote herself to so difficult a task.

Mr. Carver lived and worked in a dusty, dingy, dreary house near Mercery Lane. His rooms were above—he was a bachelor, dry and crusty—and his offices below. Two clerks, as lean as their master, worked in the dismal outer office, and in the inner apartment, the window of which looked on to a mews, Mr. Carver sat all day, and often far into the night. The appearance of so charming and blooming a woman as Dora quite lighted up the musty, fusty den. Her fresh beauty had little effect upon Carver, who regarded women as the root of all evil. The generally accepted root of all evil is money. This he approved of and hoarded; but women—he could not bear them, save in the light of clients, and then they gave him endless trouble.

"Mr. Carver," said Dora, facing the saturnine lawyer on the other side of the table, "I have called to see you about my financial position. I was, as you know, a ward of Mr. Edermont's"—Carver nodded—"and he has left me the Red House and two hundred a year." Mr. Carver nodded again. "But what about my own income of five hundred a year?"

"What five hundred a year?" said Carver grimly.

"The income which was left me by my parents."

"I was not aware that any income had been left to you by your parents, nor, for the matter of that—if you will excuse me—was I aware that you had any parents."

"What do you mean, sir?" asked Dora, sitting up very straight.

"Why," said the lawyer meditatively, "it is not hard for you to gather my meaning. I never saw your parents—I never heard mention of them. All I know is that my late client arrived here with you, and shortly after his arrival purchased the Red House. You were then a year old, and as twenty years have now elapsed, it makes you twenty-one," added Mr. Carver in parenthesis. "My late client said that you were an orphan, Carew by name, whom he intended to bring up; but as to parents, or history, or income—I know nothing about them, absolutely nothing."

"But Mr. Edermont assured me that I had five hundred a year of my own!" stammered Dora, taken aback by this plain speaking. "He handed me money from time to time, and stated frequently that he was saving the rest of the income to give me when I came of age. If this is so, I ought to be entitled to at least eight thousand pounds."

"I congratulate you on your logical arguments, and on your business capabilities," said Carver with grave irony; "but I am afraid that you are mistaken, or else that the late Mr. Edermont deceived you wilfully—a thing which I can hardly believe. I know all the details of my late client's monetary affairs. As I said before, I purchased for him the Red House freehold some twenty years ago—shortly after his arrival in the neighbourhood. The two hundred per annum which you inherit under the will is the rental of three farms, which I purchased at a later period for him. The silver, furniture and pictures, which you also inherit, he brought with him from his last dwelling-house. Finally, Miss Carew," added the lawyer, with the air of a man who is making a satisfactory statement, "I know precisely how he invested that fifty thousand pounds which, by the will, has been so foolishly offered as a reward for the discovery of the murderer of the testator. All these matters I can explain and prove, but as regards your supposititious income of five hundred pounds, I know nothing. There are," concluded Mr. Carver calmly, "neither letters, nor scrip, nor documents of any kind whatsoever among the papers of my late client which can in the least substantiate your statement, or even hint at the possibility of such a thing."

Dora listened to this long speech in silent amazement. She had never contemplated the possibility of such a deception—for now it seemed plainly a deception. Why Edermont should have told so many lies, and fostered in her a belief that she was independent as regards pecuniary matters, she could not understand. Carver waited for her to argue the matter, but Dora made no attempt to do this. The lawyer's explanation was so clear and decisive that she saw no reason to doubt his honesty. Besides, he had been always well-disposed towards her, and no motive could exist to induce him to deceive her.

"Then I am penniless?" she murmured in dismay. "Mr. Edermont deceived me!"

"Apparently he did deceive you," assented Mr. Carver, placing the tips of his fingers together; "but if you will permit me to remind you, Miss Carew, you are not penniless."

"I have a roof to cover me, and two hundred a year," said Dora bitterly. "True enough, Mr. Carver. But such a legacy is saddled with the constant companionship of Mr. Joad."

"He is scarcely a pleasant companion for a young lady, I grant, Miss Carew. But if you permit him to potter about the library and garden, I hardly think that he will trouble you much. These bookworms, dry-as-dust scholars, are so wrapped up in their books, that they rarely deign to notice mundane affairs, or the presence of youth and beauty."

Dora had her own opinion as to Mr. Joad's blindness in this direction; but as the subject was not pertinent to the matter under discussion, she made no remark on Carver's speech. After a few moments' thought, she looked earnestly at the lawyer.

"You are not deceiving me, Mr. Carver?" she asked imploringly.

"I deceive no one, Miss Carew," he replied stiffly. "If you doubt my integrity, you can consult any solicitor you think fit, and send him to me. I can prove all my statements by means of documents signed by my late client."

"It is very hard to be so deceived, Mr. Carver."

"I grant it, I grant it," said Carver hastily; "but if you wish to be rich, I can only remind you that fifty thousand pounds is waiting for the discoverer of my late client's assassin."

"I wonder you do not earn it yourself," said Dora, rising to take her leave.

"I would willingly do so, Miss Carew, but unfortunately my knowledge of Mr. Edermont's past is confined to dry business details. I do not know the romance of his life," added Carver with emphasis. "And from the romance, whatever it was, this present trouble springs."

"Do you mean a love romance?"

Carver shrugged his shoulders.

"Why not?" he said, in his dryest tone. "With all due respect to you, Miss Carew, I believe that a woman is to be found at the bottom of everything. Trace back Mr. Edermont's life to his period of romance, and you will find a woman. Find that woman, Miss Carew; learn her story, and her influence on your late guardian. Then I'll guarantee you will discover the assassin of the Red House."

Dora said nothing, but hastily took leave. But once outside, Carver's words recurred to her. They seemed to fit in with her suspicions of Lady Burville.

CHAPTER X

DR. SCOTT IS STILL OBSTINATE

Having failed with the grim lawyer, Dora resolved to see Allen. She felt singularly lonely, and longed to have some person to advise her. That should have been Allen's office, but after his cruel behaviour, Dora could scarcely bring herself to consult him. Yet it was imperative she should do so. She was an orphan, and had been kept so secluded by the selfishness of Mr. Edermont that she had not a friend in the world. If Allen failed her, the poor girl felt she would not know what to do, or who to consult. He must love her, notwithstanding his conduct, she thought; and perhaps if she told him how lonely she was, how unhappy, how greatly in need of his counsel, he might soften towards her. As Dora was naturally a haughty and self-reliant young woman, it may be guessed how isolated she felt when she so far unbent her pride as to turn for sympathy and consolation to the man who had scorned her. But, after all, she was only a woman, and subject to the weakness of her sex.

It was with slow and hesitating steps that she sought the house of her lover. She was well aware that she would find him at home at this hour; and the thought that she would soon see him face to face brought the blood to her cheeks. Pausing at the door, she twice or thrice resolved to go away; but the memory of her isolation, of her need of sympathy, confirmed her original intention. She rang the bell, and the door was opened by Mrs. Tice, who changed colour at the sight of the girl.

"Deary me, Miss Carew!" she said in some confusion; "I had no idea it was you. Is it the doctor you wish to see?"

"Yes, Mrs. Tice. Is he within?

"He is, my dear young lady. Come into the sitting-room, miss, and I'll inquire if Mr. Allen will see you."

Left alone in the room, Dora sank into a chair. The ceremony with which she had been received, the obvious confusion of Mrs. Tice, touched her painfully. She wondered what could be the reason of such things. They made her only the more determined to see Allen, and demand an explanation. But he had refused her once before; it was probable he would do so again. She felt her helpless condition keenly at this moment.

While she was thus taken up with these sad thoughts, she heard a firm step approach the door; it opened, and Allen stood before her. He seemed even more haggard and worn than the last time she had seen him. His shoulders were bent, his eyes lacked fire; altogether the man looked so thoroughly ill, so consumed by trouble and vexation of spirit, that Dora involuntarily took a step forward out of sheer sympathy. Then she recollected his conduct, and stopped short. They both looked steadily at one another.

"Why have you come to see me?" said Allen wearily. "It can do no good. I can explain nothing."

"Allen, you loved me once."

"I love you still," he responded hastily. "I shall always love you."

"Words, words, words!" said Dora, after the manner of Hamlet. "Your actions prove otherwise. Now listen to me, Allen: I have come to you for advice."

"I am the worst person in the world to give it to you," replied Scott, with cruel emphasis on the last words. "But if you wish it, I will do so."

"I do wish it, Allen. I am an orphan. I have few acquaintances, and no friends. My guardian is dead, and in all the world there is no living soul who cares about me."

"Dora!" he cried in a tone of agony, "how can you speak so? I care! I would rather die than see you suffer."

"I do not wish you to die," answered the girl with some bitterness; "it is so easy to say so—so difficult, so difficult to do. No, Allen; I wish you to live and help me. Let me put my position before you. My guardian told me that I had five hundred a year. He deceived me; I inherited nothing from my parents."

"Who told you this, Dora?"

"Mr. Carver, the lawyer. For some reason Mr. Edermont lied to me, and confirmed his lie by paying me certain moneys which he said came from my inherited income. I hear now that I am a pauper. But for his bequest of two hundred a year and the freehold of the Red House, I should be a beggar."

"I cannot understand his reason for deceiving you," said Allen, drawing a long breath; "but at all events, he has made some reparation by leaving you enough to live on. You will always have a home at the Red House."

"You do not know the conditions of the will," was Dora's reply. "I have to live at the Red House; I have to permit Mr. Joad to carry on his former life, which means that I must see him daily, and I hate the man," added Dora fervently; "I loathe him; and now that Mr. Edermont is dead, I do not know to what length his audacity may carry him."

"What do you mean?" demanded Allen, frowning.

"I mean that Joad admires me."

"Admires you?" The young man stepped forward and clenched his fists. "Impossible that he should dare!"

"Oh, trust a woman's instinct in such matters, Allen! Yes, Mr. Joad admires me, and I believe he will soon put his admiration into words."

"If he does, I'll thrash him within an inch of his life!"

"As my affianced husband you no doubt have the right," replied Dora steadily; "but have you the will? You say you love me, yet——"

"I do love you!" he burst out; "and it is because of my love for you that I keep silent. On that fatal day Edermont, beside himself with terror, betrayed to me a secret he had better have kept hidden. That secret parts us for ever. I dare not marry you."

"You dare not? What secret can have the power to make you say such words?"

"If I told you that, I should tell you all," replied Allen sullenly. "Do not try me beyond my strength, Dora. If you suffer, I suffer also. For your own sake I keep silent, and I love you too dearly to inflict unnecessary pain."

"What you might inflict can be no worse than what you have inflicted," said Dora bitterly. "I see it is useless to ask you to confide in me. But one word: has this secret to do with Mr. Edermont's death?"

Allen hesitated; then, turning away his head:

"I cannot answer you," he said resolutely.

"Oh!" said Dora in a taunting tone; "then you know something about the death."

"I know nothing," replied Allen, with a white face.

"Yes, you do. Your refusal to explain shows me that the secret has to do with the murder. Perhaps Mr. Edermont told you the name of the person he was afraid of. Well, that person perhaps carried out his wicked purpose."

"Why do you say 'perhaps'?" asked Allen suddenly. "You seem to be doubtful."

"Because a day or two before the crime was committed, Mr. Pallant called on my guardian. What he told him relieved him of the fear of assassination. Therefore I do not know if Mr. Edermont's enemy killed him."

Allen jumped up and looked eagerly at the girl.

"Did Pallant say that the person whom Mr. Edermont feared was—was dead?"

"I cannot answer you that. Mr. Edermont only said that his nightmare was at an end. I presume from such a speech that he felt there was no more danger. Unfortunately, he was murdered shortly afterwards, so that his hopes were vain. But you apparently know all about this person whom my guardian feared. What is his name?"

"I can't tell you, Dora," said Allen with a groan.

"Oh, I do not want you to tell me!" she replied scornfully, "but tell the authorities. No doubt you will be rewarded with fifty thousand pounds—blood-money."

"Dora! How can you speak like this to me?"

"How else do you wish me to speak?" she retorted fiercely. "Do you think that I have water in my veins, to put up with your neglect in silence?"

"It is for your own good."

"You should permit me to be the best judge of that, Allen. My brain is in confusion from the event of last week. I have suffered indescribably. With Lady Burville and her fainting in church came disaster. That woman caused a breach between us——"

"No, no! Lady Burville has nothing to do with my secret."

"Will you deny that her name was mentioned several times between you and Mr. Edermont?"

"No, I will not deny it," he returned doggedly. "All the same, she has nothing to do with the matter."

"So you say, for the preservation of your secret," said Dora disdainfully; "but I believe that she has everything to do with the matter. And what is more," continued the girl, raising her voice, "I feel assured that indirectly she caused the death of my guardian."

Allen turned even paler than before.

"I assure you such is not the case, Dora."

"I decline to take your word for it. I will only believe the evidence of my own senses, of my own researches."

"Your own researches?"

"Yes; I intend to find out this secret which is a bar to our marriage. To do so I must solve the mystery of Mr. Edermont's death."

"I warn you not to do so;" cried Allen, breathing heavily; "you are playing with fire!"

"I'll take the risk of that—if risk there is. Allen," she said, placing her hands on his shoulders, "you laughed at my premonition of evil when I spoke to you of Lady Burville. You see I was right. Now I have a premonition of good. My researches will mend the breach between us, and bring about our marriage."

"Impossible! and, moreover——" he hesitated. "Can you love me after the cruel way in which I have been forced to behave to you?"

"Yes. You mention the poison and the antidote at once. You have been cruel, but you have been forced, as I truly believe, to be so. When I discover that force, I shall learn the bar to our marriage. If so, it can be removed."

"I am afraid not," he replied, shaking his head.

"In the meantime," she continued, as though she had not heard him, "as I am a pauper, I must remain at the Red House. But I refuse to do so in the company of that creature Joad, unless I have a companion. Will you let Mrs. Tice come and stay with me for a few weeks?"

"If Mrs. Tice will go, I shall be delighted that you should have her."

"Very good, Allen." She rose from her chair. "Now we understand one another. When I know the truth, I shall come and see you again. Till then, we must be strangers."

"I suppose so," said Scott gloomily; "but I warn you the danger is great when you know the truth——"

"Well, what will be the result?"

Allen Scott looked at her pityingly.

"Your life will be ruined, as mine has been," he said.

Dora walked towards the window with a weary sigh.

"It is ruined already; I do not see how it can be much worse. I have lost you; I have been deceived as regards my pecuniary position; I am threatened with the attentions of that odious creature. It is all very terrible."

Allen groaned.

"I wish I could give you hope, Dora, but I cannot. I see nothing in the future but pain, and separation, and misery."

"Oh, I don't know," replied Dora with a hard laugh. "Since you can give me up so easily, I have no doubt that you will speedily console yourself for my loss. You will be married in a few years."

"Never! If I do not marry you—and that is impossible—I shall marry no other woman."

"So you say; but I know what men are."

"Not from experience."

"I don't think a woman needs experience to divine the nature of the other sex," said Dora loftily, with all the brave self-confidence of youth; "our instinct teaches us what you are and how you will act. I can't expect you to be true to a phantom all your life."

"Phantom! You are flesh and blood, my dear."

"Yes; but I mean that should I fail to discover this secret, or should you persist in treating me as a child, we must part, and never see one another again. I will then be nothing to you but a phantom—a memory. No man can remain true to a memory."

"Strange as it may appear to you, Dora, there have been men thus faithful, and I swear——"

"Do not swear fidelity. You will only perjure yourself in after years. But it is no use discussing such things, my dear," she continued more cheerfully. "I must return home."

"Will you come back and see me again?"

"If I have occasion to, I shall do so. I do not intend to part from you until all mysteries are made plain. It shall be my business to make them so."

"A hopeless task," sighed Allen, as he accompanied her to the door. "I shall send Mrs. Tice over to you in the morning."

"Thank you. Do you know that Mrs. Tice was once acquainted with my guardian?"

"Yes; she said something about it," he murmured, turning away his head; "she knows something."

"I am convinced of that. She knows the celebrated past of Mr. Edermont, about which so much has been said. I would not be surprised if she knew the contents of that stolen manuscript."

"I dare say; but she may not know everything."

"She knows more than you give her credit for," said Dora dryly. "For instance; when you returned from London, I dare say she knew why you had gone there."

"Yes; that's true enough."

"And she knew why you quarrelled with my guardian."

"She did. What of that?"

"Only this," said Miss Carew triumphantly; "Mr. Carver said that he believed the past whence this present trouble arose was connected with a woman in love with Mr. Edermont. For all I know, that woman may be—Mrs. Tice."

CHAPTER XI

PREPARING THE GROUND

When Dora returned to the Red House, she made up her mind. Since Allen refused to tell her his secret, she would discover it herself, and judge if it were as serious a bar to their marriage as he asserted. She did not think for a moment that Allen knew who had killed Edermont, but she could not help concluding that he was aware of something likely to lead to the identification of the assassin. Perhaps he knew the story of Edermont's life, set forth in the manuscript which had been stolen from the bureau by the murderer. But whatever knowledge he was possessed of, Dora saw plainly enough that he was resolved to hold his peace. The truth is, she was afraid to admit his motive for silence even to herself. She half guessed the reason of his determination, but she neither spoke nor thought about it.

There were two ways in which she could go to work; either begin from the arrival of Lady Burville at Hernwood Hall, and progress onward to the committal of the crime, or begin from the fact of the murder, and trace back its motive to Lady Burville. After some consideration, she decided on the latter of these two courses. But Lady Burville had departed, and Dora was ignorant of her present address. Even if she did learn it, there was no excuse whereby she could gain an interview with the lady. She had no proof that this stranger was implicated in the crime, and if she were—a fact which Dora fully believed—there would be little chance of forcing her into confession. This course was therefore out of the question, but there remained the other. Starting with the evidence which had gathered round the crime itself, the theories, the suppositions, the beliefs, Dora thought she might piece together scattered hints and facts, which might be woven into a rope strong enough to hang the assassin. But the difficulty, in the absence of all absolute knowledge, was to discover the criminal.

And there was yet another thing to be remembered. The reward of fifty thousand pounds had brought into competition hundreds of men, bent upon gaining the prize. From far and near they came to Canterbury, and haunted the environs of the Red House. But not one of them entered the gates, for these were kept locked, and the famous postern through which the assassin had passed had been bricked up, by Dora's order. Every labourer and tramp and shopkeeper in the neighbourhood was questioned and cross-questioned by these pests, but none gained any information likely to solve the mystery. No trace could be found of Edermont's past life. He had appeared in the place twenty years before; he had bought the Red House, and a few farms; he had lived in retirement since that time. Beyond this nothing could be learned, and, notwithstanding the magnitude of the reward, no one was fortunate enough to make a step forward. Out of the night the assassin had come, into the night he had gone; and neither Inspector Jedd nor the many amateur detectives could trace him to his hiding-place. Hemmed in by these difficulties on all sides, with no information to go upon, with obstinate people like Joad, Allen, and Mrs. Tice to deal with, it can be easily seen how difficult was the problem which Dora wished to solve. On surveying the situation her heart failed her; she felt helpless.

One chance she had of making a beginning, and that was by questioning Joad as to the motive of the crime. That this motive was to be found in Edermont's past life Dora was certain; and as Joad was more likely than anyone else to know that past, he would be the proper person to apply to for information. From conversations which she had overheard, Dora was satisfied that the secret of the horror which had overshadowed Edermont's life—which had sent him to church and to the consolation of the Litany—was known to Joad. And as Joad evinced a decided admiration for her, she resolved to use such admiration for the purpose of discovering the truth. When she learned the secret of Edermont's past, she would learn the name of the person he dreaded; that name would identify the assassin, and if she found the assassin she might be able to learn and do away with the unknown obstacle to her marriage with Allen. She would gain also the fortune of the dead man; but that, in Dora's opinion, was a side issue.

In the meantime, and before she had time to formulate her plans—which, indeed, were but in their inception—Mrs. Tice came over, bag and baggage, to play the part of dragon at the Red House. Dora was glad to welcome her within its walls; not only because she promised to stand a bulwark of respectability against Joad, but also because Mrs. Tice might reveal by accident something of Edermont's past. The conversation at Canterbury had shown Dora very plainly that some time or another Mrs. Tice had been acquainted with the recluse; and that such acquaintance must have been prior to his purchase of the Red House. At that period had been engendered the terror which had haunted the poor creature, and Mrs. Tice might have some inkling of its nature.

The old housekeeper, however, was not to be cajoled into

reminiscences of the past. She kept a guard over her tongue, and resolutely avoided all Dora's hints and significant remarks. It was quite a week before Dora could induce her to converse on the subject at all, and then she spoke in an ambiguous fashion. Life at that moment seemed to Dora to resemble a theatre with the curtain down. If she could induce Mrs. Tice to raise the curtain, what shadowy drama of the past might not be performed! Seven days after the arrival of Mrs. Tice she lifted the curtain a little—a very little—but revealed enough to excite the liveliest curiosity in the girl.

It was after nine o'clock, and as usual Joad had been turned out to have his supper, and talk classics with Mr. Pride, the schoolmaster. The gates were locked, the shutters of the windows were closed, and Mrs. Tice was seated in Dora's own sitting-room, with a basket of work before her. Dora sat by the one window, which had not yet been shut, and the pale light of the evening floated into the room, to mingle with the dim radiance of the solitary candle which illuminated the busy fingers of the housekeeper. Meg Gance was in her kitchen, resting after the labours of the day, so the two women were quite alone. Suddenly Dora yawned, and stretched out her hands.

"Heigh-ho!" said she in a wearied tone. "How long is this going on, I wonder?"

"What are you referring to, Miss Carew?" asked the housekeeper in her pleasant voice—"to your life here?"

"Yes; to my lonely and miserable life. I feel simply wretched."

"Do not say that, my dear young lady. You have health, and youth, and many blessings."

"No doubt," replied Dora scornfully; "but I have lost the chief of my blessings."

"You mean Mr. Allen?" said the old lady in an embarrassed tone.

"Yes, I do, Mrs. Tice. And since he has left me, I do not see why I should not accept the attentions of Mr. Lambert Joad. The wretched old man worships the ground I walk on."

"Of course you are jesting?" said Mrs. Tice, with an uneasy smile; "but I see that Mr. Joad admires you. More's the pity."

"Why 'more's the pity'?"

"Well, you see, miss, he will not relish your rebuffing him for his impertinence; and he is likely to prove a dangerous enemy."

"Pshaw! He can do me no harm."

"I am not so sure of that, miss. He knows a good deal about Mr. Edermont's past life."

Dora turned round and looked sharply at the comely, withered face.

"Is there anything in the past life of Mr. Edermont likely to be harmful to me?"

"Yes," said Mrs. Tice deliberately, "there is."

"And do you know what it is?"

"Yes, miss; I know what it is, and so does Mr. Allen. It was a knowledge of that past which sent him up to London. Since he returned we have talked over the matter, and we have both concluded that it is best to hold our tongues. But if Mr. Joad knows the secret, and you rebuff him, he may not be wise enough to keep silent."

"I am glad to hear you say so!" cried Dora with animation. "Since I can learn the secret from no one else, I'll see if a rebuff cannot loosen Mr. Joad's tongue."

"If you are wise, you will let well alone," warned Mrs. Tice, feeling that she had said too much.

Dora crossed the room, and stood with her hands behind her back, looking indignantly at the old woman.

"Upon my word, it is a shame!" she said in a low voice. "I am apparently surrounded by pitfalls on all sides, yet no one will tell me how to avoid them."

"If you remain quiet, you won't fall into them," replied Mrs. Tice with a nod.

"Quiet!" cried Dora, frowning. "Good heavens! how can I remain quiet when I see my life falling into ruins? No, no, no!" She stamped her foot defiantly. "I must act, I must inquire, I must know what all these mysteries mean!"

"You will never arrive at that knowledge, Miss Carew."

"I'm not so sure of that, Mrs. Tice. Remember your hint about that Joad creature. I'll wring it out of him, if I can't out of anyone else. Mrs. Tice"—Dora flung herself on her knees before the housekeeper—"did you know Mr. Edermont before he came to the Red House?"

"Yes, Miss Carew, I can admit that much: I knew Mr. Edermont."

"Was that when you were Allen's nurse?"

"Yes, Miss Carew."

"In the service of Allen's parents?"

"I was in the service of Dr. and Mrs. Scott," replied Mrs. Tice composedly. "Pray don't ask me any more questions, Miss Carew, for I cannot answer them."

"You will not, you mean," said Dora, rising. "Never mind, I have found out something from the little you have told me."

Mrs. Tice looked up quickly.

"Impossible," she said anxiously. "I have revealed nothing."

"Oh, I can put two and two together, Mrs. Tice," said Dora quietly. "Allen told me that his parents lived in Christchurch, Hants—that his father and mother are buried there. Now, if you knew Mr. Edermont while you were nursing Allen, Mr. Edermont must have lived, or have been on a visit, at Christchurch. Consequently, if I go down to Christchurch I shall learn something of Mr. Edermont's past life."

Mrs. Tice fell into the skilfully-laid trap.

"You won't find that the name of Edermont is known in those parts," she said, without thinking.

"Precisely," said Dora coolly. "Edermont is a false name. I have suspected that for some time. Thank you, Mrs. Tice, for admitting it. I have learnt so much from you. Mr. Joad will tell me the rest."

"Mr. Joad may or may not," said Mrs. Tice doubtfully. "Do not go too much by what I am saying, Miss Carew. You have a skilful and crafty person to deal with."

"Are you talking of yourself?"

"By no means. I am neither skilful nor crafty. I allude to Mr. Joad."

"You seem to be well acquainted with his character, Mrs. Tice. Did you know him at Christchurch?"

"No, my dear. I never saw the man until I came here—to this house. But I have eyes in my head, and I can see that he is singularly deceitful."

"Perhaps, but harmless."

Mrs. Tice shook her head with pursed-up lips.

"I disagree with you. The adder is harmless so long as it isn't trodden upon. Tread upon Mr. Joad, my dear young lady, and he will—bite."

To emphasize the last word Mrs. Tice snapped off a piece of thread, and looked up at Dora with a sharp nod. Evidently Joad had failed to impress her favourably.

"I have no doubt you are right," said Dora, after reflection. "He would be dangerous if he got the chance, but I don't see where his opportunity for mischief comes in."

"Neither do I, Miss Carew; but he'll watch for one, you mark my words."

Dora did not reply to this remark, as she was of the same opinion herself. She was thinking about Carver's remark touching a past romance of Edermont's, and of her own statement to Allen that Mrs. Tice might have been the woman who had to do with the same. It was now her desire to find out if there was any grain of truth in her supposition, but she did not know exactly how to put it to Mrs.

Tice. At last she thought the best method to approach so delicate a subject was by a side issue.

"Your husband is dead, isn't he, Mrs. Tice?" she asked with apparent carelessness.

"Yes, Miss Carew," replied the housekeeper; "he died more than twenty-five years ago, and his body is buried in the graveyard of Christchurch Priory."

"Were you much in love with him?"

"We respected and liked one another," said Mrs. Tice judiciously: "but we were not madly in love."

"Were you ever madly in love with anyone, Mrs. Tice?"

"No, my dear young lady," was the laughing reply, "never! I am not a romantic person."

Dora thought for a moment.

"Was Mr. Edermont handsome when you knew him first?"

"He was passable, Miss Carew—a little, womanish man. Even in his youth his hair was white—the effect of nerves, I believe. He was always nervous, poor soul!"

"He had reason to be, evidently."

"Yes," said Mrs. Tice sharply, "good reason. I never liked him, but I was sorry for him."

Determined to know the exact truth, Dora put her question plainly:

"Were you in love with him?"

"What!" said Mrs. Tice, laughing, "with that rat of a man? No, my dear: I had better taste."

This was conclusive, and Dora was satisfied that, whoever had played the part of heroine in her guardian's romance, it was not Mrs. Tice.

CHAPTER XII

A TERRIBLE ACCUSATION

The next day Dora altered her demeanour towards Joad. Hitherto she had been cold and unapproachable; now she sought his society with smiles, and quite bewildered the poor man with kindness. If Joad, who was naturally very crafty, had not been in love, he would have mistrusted this sudden transformation and been on his guard. As it was, in the then state of his feelings, he ascribed Dora's changed behaviour to a desire to be on better terms with one who was bound, owing to the terms of the will, to come into contact daily with her. In this belief he reciprocated her advances, and vied with her in amiability.

On her part, Mrs. Tice viewed the comedy with displeasure. Nevertheless, she made no attempt to interfere. Although she was unwilling to be an active party in revealing the truth to Dora, yet she was by no means displeased that the girl should learn it from a third person. Dora was deeply in love with Allen; and the sooner she realized that there could be no union between them, the better it would be. To come to such an understanding, it was necessary that she should learn the secret. When she was possessed of such knowledge, the housekeeper was satisfied that, even if Dr. Scott did desire the match, Dora would refuse her consent thereto. Therefore Mrs. Tice preferred being spectator to actor. For some days Dora pursued her amiable tactics, and Joad fell deep and deeper in love. He was well aware, in his own heart, that this girl, young enough to be his granddaughter, would never consent to be his wife; but for all that, he put no restraint upon his feelings. Moreover, he had a weapon in his hand which he hoped to use with effect. In spite of his belief that Dora might not accept him voluntarily, he fancied that he could force her into the match by making use of the weapon aforesaid. But it was not to be brought into active service save as a last resource.

Meanwhile the comedy of May and December, of Methuselah in Arcady, of "An Old Man's Darling," went gaily on. Joad paid more attention to his dress, he drank less brandy, and talked more affably. Instead of burying himself in the library, he was to be found haunting the steps of Dora. He loved her very shadow, and was never tired of gazing at her face. She seemed to him to be the most beautiful, the most wonderful, the most gracious woman in the world; and he gloated over her charms like an old satyr. Crafty, astute and worldly as he was, he fell prostrate at her feet, a debased Merlin entangled in the wiles of an artificial Vivien.

Dora played her part bravely; but at times it was too much for her, and she would leave the house to scour the country on her bicycle. Joad was too old and shaky to accompany her, and she was thus relieved in some measure from his senile adoration. But, however near she approached to Canterbury, she never entered the town or sought out Allen.

"No," she said to herself, when unusually impelled to make the visit; "first I shall learn the truth. Once in possession of Allen's secret, of the name of Mr. Edermont's assassin, and I shall know how to act; till then I shall remain absent."

But, with all her diplomacy, it was not so easy to gain the confidence of Joad. The least hint at Mr. Edermont's past, and he withdrew into himself. He evaded her most dexterous inquiries; and when she pressed him hard, assumed the character of a dull, stupid old man who knew nothing about the matter. Yet he was not unwilling to discuss the details of the murder and subsequent robbery, although he professed himself unable to account for either. By acting thus, he ignored the question of Edermont's secret enemy.

But one day Dora succeeded in forcing him into plain speaking; but the revelation made was one she was far from expecting. The beginning of the whole matter lay in the fact that she discovered Joad in the library the worse for drink. It was not that he was confused or maudlin, for the man's brain and speech were both clear. But he was filled with Dutch courage, which made him more audacious than usual. Dora reproved him for his vice.

"You should be ashamed of yourself, drinking so much brandy, Mr. Joad!" she said severely.

"I have not touched brandy for weeks!" said Joad, lying glibly, after the fashion of habitual drunkards.

Dora looked at him in contempt, and pointed out a tall mirror, before which they were both standing. It reflected her own tall, straight form, and also the figure of the disreputable old sinner.

"Can you see your face and deny it?" she said in a tone of rebuke. "Your eyes are red, your clothes are awry, your——"

"Leave me to bear the burden of my own sins," said Joad sullenly; "if I take brandy, I don't ask you to pay for it."

"But you are a gentleman, a scholar," persisted Dora, sorry for the wretched old creature; "you should be above such low vices."

"We cannot be above the depths to which we have fallen, Miss Carew. My life has been one long failure, so it is scarcely to be wondered at that I fly to drink for consolation. Few men have been so hardly treated as I have been."

"Yet Mr. Edermont helped you."

"No doubt," retorted Joad viciously; "but he would not have stretched out a finger to save me if I had not forced him to."

"You forced Mr. Edermont to——?"

"I forced him to nothing," interrupted Joad, seeing that he had gone too far. "It is only my way of speaking. Don't mind the ramblings of a foolish old failure."

Dora looked at him silently. His eyes were filled with tears, and, ashamed of betraying his emotion, he turned away to busy himself with dusting a book. In the few words which he had let slip Dora saw that he had possessed some power over the dead man which had won him house and home. That power she believed was connected with the lifelong misery of Edermont, and with the fact of his murder. The idea made her take an unexpected step. Seizing the astonished Joad by the arm, she whirled him round, so as to look straight into his eyes.

"Did you kill Mr. Edermont?" she asked abruptly. Joad looked at her in amazement, and sneered in her face.

"O Lord! Have you got that idea into your head?" said he contemptuously. "No, Miss Carew, I did not kill Mr. Edermont. One does not readily kill the goose with the golden eggs. By Julian's death I have lost a protector—almost a home. Do you take me for a fool?"

"I take you for a man who knows more than he says," said Dora tartly.

"Then I am wise. I keep my own counsel until the time comes for me to speak."

"I do not understand you."

"You will some day," retorted Joad with a leer, "and that sooner than you expect. I wonder at your accusing me of this crime," he continued in an injured tone. "By your own evidence the murder took place at one o'clock, and at that time I was talking to Mr. Pride in my cottage. I wonder at your talking like this, Miss Carew."

"I beg your pardon, Mr. Joad," said Dora ceremoniously. "I know that you proved an alibi. There is one thing about you that I admire," she added, after a pause.

Joad's eyes glittered like stars as he turned an admiring glance in the direction of the young girl, and bent forward eagerly.

"What is that?" he demanded.

"You do not care for money."

"No," said Joad, after a pause; "I do not care particularly for money. As long as I have a roof, a crust, and my books, I am satisfied. My wants are simple. But why," he continued, looking at her in a puzzled way, "why do you make such a remark?"

"Because you refuse to pocket fifty thousand pounds."

"You allude to the reward. My dear lady, I cannot gain that."

"I am not so sure of your inability to do so," said Dora coolly. "With your knowledge of Mr. Edermont's past life, you must know who it was he feared. If you know the name of that person, you know who killed him. With that knowledge, why not apply for the fifty thousand pounds?"

"I am not so omniscient as you think, Miss Carew. But we will suppose, for the sake of argument, that I have such knowledge: what would it benefit me to gain this fortune?"

"You could do good with it."

"Could I gain your love?"

Dora turned away with a flushed face, feeling the delicacy of the position.

"You must not talk to me like that, Mr. Joad," she said with great dignity.

"Why not? I love you."

"Then you ought to be ashamed to say so. I am the affianced wife of another man."

"Allen Scott?"

"Yes," said Dora with emphasis, "Dr. Allen Scott.

"Bah! Why should you think of him? Has he stood by you in this trouble? Not he! He left you to fight the matter out by yourself. Besides, there are reasons why you should not marry him."

Dora's heart beat rapidly. Was she about to learn the truth? Had her rebuff brought about the desired result, and would this old man reveal what so long had been hidden? She believed that such was the case, and could scarcely manage, so intense was her excitement, to ask the necessary question to lure him on to a full confession. However, by an effort of will she managed to keep her voice fairly steady.

"Are there any special reasons that you know of?"

"Several!" snarled Joad, rubbing his hands together, with an evil glitter in his eyes.

"I should be glad to hear them," she said in the tone of an empress.

"I dare say you would; but I don't intend to tell you what they are."

"Why not?" demanded Dora, trying to hide her disappointment at this unlooked-for result.

"Because I don't choose to speak until it is my pleasure to do so," said Joad insolently. "Oh, I can see what you are up to, Miss

Carew. You are trying to force the truth out of me for purposes of your own. But you shan't—shan't—shan't!"

The old creature stamped with rage, and his face grew so red in his excitement that Dora really thought he was about to have a fit. She looked at him in astonishment, while he strove to control his anger and assume a dignified demeanour. Such conduct was not to be tolerated, and Dora walked towards the door of the library.

"I shall return when you know how to conduct yourself," she said coldly.

Before she could open the door the delinquent shuffled after her, in a state of childish repentance. "Do not go, do not go!" he cried piteously. "I am very sorry; indeed, I am very sorry."

"Then why do you talk such nonsense?" said Dora, seeing that she had gained an advantage. "Do you think I want to know your secrets, you foolish old man?"

"Yes, yes; I am a foolish old man," he repeated, catching up her words eagerly; "but do not be angry with me. I love you. Oh, Dora, dear, sweet Dora, I love you!" and whining in this fashion the old man fell on his knees.

"Rise, Mr. Joad! Do not be foolish. Get up at once—I insist!"

"Not until you promise to be my wife. I love you. I am old, but my heart is young. Listen, listen!" he continued, glancing round. "If you want money, I can get fifty thousand pounds. I know who killed Julian!"

Dora tore her dress from his grasp in horror. "You know who killed Mr. Edermont!"

"Yes; I will tell the name; I will gain the fortune; I will give it to you. Only consent to be my wife."

"Your wife!" cried Dora, shrinking back with visible repugnance.

"Ah, I know that I am old," said Joad piteously, "but reflect. There is much to be gained by you. I cannot live long; you would soon be my widow. I would leave you all the money; and think how rich you would be!"

"I wouldn't marry you if you offered me millions!" said Dora with contempt. "I love one man only, and him only shall I marry."

Joad rose in a fury. "Don't tell me his name!" he shrieked; "I know it. Allen—that miserable wretch! But you shall never marry him—never!"

"How can you prevent our marriage?"

"By telling the truth—by gaining the fortune!" He stepped forward and seized her wrist. "I hold the life of your lover in the hollow of my hand!"

"What do you mean?" panted Dora. "Explain!"

"You wish to know my secrets. Well, I shall tell you one—one only—that will make your heart sore and your face white. Who killed Julian? Who came here in the dead of night and struck his foul blow? Who but Allen Scott—Allen Scott, the murderer! Curse him!"

CHAPTER XIII

DENIAL

This, then, was the weapon which Joad had reserved to strike his last blow. By denouncing Scott he hoped to win a fortune; but by keeping silent for Dora's sake he thought he could force her to marry him. In either case he stood to win. With his indifference to money, he preferred the girl to the fifty thousand pounds. It only remained for her to accept his hand, in order to save her lover from death on the gallows. But as yet this was doubtful. Certainly the bolt had been shot; but would the bolt fall? He waited.

With fixed eyes and bloodless face, Dora retreated slowly backwards. At length she reached the wall, and leant against it, overcome with mingled feelings of terror and astonishment. Joad, his hands hanging loosely by his sides, stood looking at her, with a doubtful smile on his pale lips. Seeing that she did not speak, he repeated his accusation in a different form. He was now calmer.

"Your lover is the murderer of your guardian," said he, watching the effect of each word.

Something in the malice of his tones brought back the courage to Dora's heart with a rush. She flushed up bravely, and stepped forward boldly. Joad did not move, and she came close to him—so close that he could feel her breath on his withered cheek. For a final taunt he spoke again.

"A murderer—that fine young man—your lover! Just think of it!"

"You lie!" She brought out the words coldly, and without the least display of passion. Knowing Scott as she did, the charge was so monstrous that she could hardly forbear from breaking into hysterical laughter. As it was, she controlled herself admirably, and merely repeated her words. "You lie, Mr. Joad," she said steadily. "Your accusation springs from malice. You cannot substantiate your lie."

Without wasting time in asseverations, Joad simply raised his finger to emphasize his words. He related without preamble the grounds upon which he based his accusation.

"Listen," he said, in his rich, deep voice; "you remember that day on which you brought Scott to see Julian. Very good. As you know, they had a serious quarrel. You heard yourself that Julian called out for protection. Scott wished to kill him at that moment."

"But why—why?" she stammered, making a vague gesture with her hand.

"Ah! you ask me more than I can tell. I was not present during the conversation, you know. However, I can guess what took place. I refuse to tell all, but this much I dare speak. Julian cast certain reflections on the dead parents of Scott; he mentioned something which took place twenty and more years ago."

"At Christchurch?" she murmured.

He looked surprised.

"I don't know who told you so much," he said brusquely, "but I admit that your information is correct. At Christchurch, Miss Carew, an episode took place which was not creditable to Dr. Scott's parents."

"Had the episode to do with Mr. Edermont?"

"I cannot tell you. I am speaking of my grounds for suspecting your lover. What passed before matters nothing. Suffice it for you to understand that Julian quarrelled with Scott, and he was afraid lest the young man should murder him. You heard his cry for help."

"Well?" said Dora, seeing that he paused.

"Well," replied Joad, with a suave smile, "he did murder him."

"No; I do not believe it. Where are your proofs?"

Joad darted an imperious glance at her shrinking form.

"I am about to produce my proofs," he declared calmly. "On the night of the second of August I left here at nine o'clock. You assisted Julian to lock the gates behind me, if I remember. I went to my cottage and had my supper. Afterwards I waited for Mr. Pride, who had promised to look in on his return from Canterbury. Ten o'clock, eleven o'clock, twelve o'clock struck, and still Pride did not come. I thought that he had arranged to stay all night in Canterbury, but shortly after twelve I went out on to the road to see if he was coming. I did not see him; I did see Dr. Scott."

"Allen?" cried Dora disbelievingly.

"Himself. He was coming down the road on a bicycle."

"How could you recognise him in the dark?"

"The moon was up. I recognised him in the moonlight."

"Did he see you?"

"No; I was standing in the shadow. I was astonished to see him near the Red House at midnight, and I watched him. He passed the gates, and got off his bicycle at the end of the wall. Then he turned down the side path which leads to the postern gate. I waited to see if he would return, but as he did not I was about to follow him, when Pride arrived. Unwilling to say anything about what I had seen, lest it should compromise your lover, I took Pride into my house, and there I got talking to him till after two o'clock. In the interest of our conversation, I quite forgot Scott and his visit. But the next morning"—he looked at her in a crafty way—"I heard of the murder, and I found the postern gate open."

"And—and what inference do you draw from all this?" murmured Dora, with white lips.

"I infer that Scott called to see Julian with reference to their previous quarrel, perhaps to demand proofs as to the episode of Christchurch. I believe that he climbed the wall and entered the house through the glass door of the drawing-room, which Julian had not locked. I have no doubt that he found Julian in his study, that Julian told him the story of the episode was locked up in the bureau. No doubt Scott insisted upon having the papers which revealed the dishonour of his parents placed in his hands. Julian would naturally refuse. Then the quarrel would recommence, and the end of it would be—well," added Joad, with a shrug, "you know the rest. Julian was killed, and the bureau robbed of that paper. What further proof can you desire that Dr. Scott murdered your guardian?"

Dora heard this story with a suffocating feeling in her throat. She felt as though a net were being thrown round Allen, as though he would be tangled in its meshes. It was true that he had returned from London on the night of the murder; but she could not understand why he should have visited the Red House at midnight. Then she remembered that Allen had gone to town on business connected with that terrible conversation with Edermont. What if he had learnt that Edermont had spoken the truth regarding the dishonour of his parents, and had returned to revenge himself on the old man? These thoughts occurred to her with lightning rapidity; but in the end they all gave place to one. She must save him at any cost; to do so she must close Joad's mouth.

"Why did you not speak of this before?" she asked in a trembling voice.

"I wished to tell you first. You know that I love you. I wish you to be my wife. If you marry me, Scott will be safe. If not——"

"If not, what would you do?"

"My duty," said he solemnly.

The situation was frightful. Dora felt that she must scream, if only to relieve the tension of her nerves. If Joad denounced Allen, the doctor would be arrested; and what defence could he make, what explanation could he give, for coming to the Red House on the night, at the very time, of the committal of the crime? She said nothing, trying to collect her thoughts, while Joad blinked at her through his half-shut eyes.

"And, after all, you couldn't marry him," he declared suddenly; "he is guilty."

"That has yet to be proved," said Dora faintly. "I cannot believe that Allen committed so horrible a crime. His motive——"

"His motive will be found in the papers he stole," said Joad brutally. "But come—your answer. Consent to be my wife, or I go to the police this evening."

"You—you must give me time," she stammered.

Joad nodded.

"That is only fair," he said gravely. "I will give you a week. If you do not promise by that time, well—your lover goes to the scaffold."

How Dora got out of the library and climbed the stairs to her own room she did not know. There was a humming in her ears, and the place seemed to go round and round. With an access of despair she threw herself on the bed, and tried to face the situation. Allen was innocent, she was certain, although no proofs of such innocence presented themselves at the moment. But, on the face of it, his conduct appeared to be suspicious. What was he doing at the Red House at midnight? Why had he come there by stealth? If Joad denounced him, Dora could see no hope of saving his life. Still, she could protect him by becoming the wife of this disreputable Silenus, whom she loathed with all her soul. But he held Allen's life in his hand, and the poor young fellow was doomed unless he could make some defence.

Defence! She sat up suddenly and thought. She had not yet heard Allen's side of the question. Perhaps he could explain himself, and give a reasonable excuse for his presence in the study at so untoward an hour. She remembered that Edermont had written asking Allen to call and see him. Might he not have appointed the conference for midnight, and have left the postern gate and the glass door open so that Allen could enter without attracting attention? All this was feasible enough, and might be put forward in his defence. But on second thoughts Dora gave way to despair. Even so straightforward a tale would be against the presumption of his innocence.

Assuming that he had been in the study at the appointed hour, how could he prove himself guiltless? The fact of the previous quarrel was known to herself and Joad. Nothing was more likely than that they might have continued their dispute. Perhaps Edermont might have threatened Allen with his pistol, and to protect himself Scott might have torn the knobkerrie from the wall. But had he struck the blow? Had he—— Dora closed her eyes with a faint cry, to shut out the vision of horror which that thought conjured into existence.

Without doubt Allen had been present in the study at the time of the murder. Joad saw him after twelve o'clock. Dora knew that the crime had been committed a minute or so before one. It was just possible that Allen had left the house before that time. But who could prove that he had so departed? Dora rose from her bed, and paced to and fro, distracted by a hundred thoughts that swarmed in her head like hiving bees.

"The murder was committed before one o'clock," she said aloud. "I can prove that. The striking of the clock came almost on top of that cry for help. Could Allen have gone away before then? He must have done. I cannot believe that he would murder an inoffensive old man. No provocation would make him commit so brutal a crime. He is cool and collected; he is not passionate and impulsive. No, no, no! Allen is innocent! He left my guardian alive and well. Allen went—but who remained?"

Had two people been present? Dora remembered that Edermont had written other letters at the same time as that to Allen. Perhaps he had invited a third person to be present at that midnight conference. If so, when Allen departed, the third person might have remained to kill Edermont and rifle the desk. If such were the case, Allen must know the name of that third person. Why, then, did he not denounce that person to the police?—not so much for the gaining of fifty thousand pounds as to accomplish an act of justice. Why was he silent? Why did he not speak out in his own defence? Dora could not but acknowledge in her own heart that the circumstantial evidence was strong against her lover.

"Oh, I can't stay here thinking—thinking!" she cried fiercely; "it will drive me mad. I shall go to Canterbury and see Allen. He must speak out now, if only to defend himself from Joad. A week—a week—seven days—and his life and my happiness to be saved in that short space of time. I must think; I must act. Oh, Allen, Allen!"

She glanced at her watch. It was close on four o'clock. If she rode into Canterbury at once, she might find Allen at home. He usually came in between four and five to have tea. No one was likely to be present, so she would have him all to herself. At once she made up her mind, and without a word to Joad or to Mrs. Tice she went out of the house. In a few minutes she was spinning along the highroad as fast as her machine could go.

Dora was right in her surmise. Allen was at home, and at tea. She went straight into the dining-room and saw him at the table. He looked up with an air of astonishment at her appearance; and, noting his pale and startled face, Dora felt a pang. Was he guilty after all, or was the terror visible in his face merely the result of her sudden entrance? Without a word, she shut the door sharply, and took a seat by the side of the table. Allen welcomed her with an air of constraint. He offered her a cup of tea and a plate of cake. Dora pushed them both away in a state of fierce excitement, leant her arms on the table, and looked at him steadily. He stared at her in surprise, marvelling at her strange behaviour.

"Allen," she said abruptly, "what were you doing at the Red House on the night of the murder?"

The young man turned even paler than before, dropped the plates he was holding, and fell into his chair as though he had been shot.

"Who—who says I was there?" he stammered.

"Mr. Joad—he accuses you."

"Accuses—acc——"—he could hardly get the words out—"accuses me—of what?"

"Of murdering Mr. Edermont. Allen, don't look at me like that. It is not true?"

"Dora," said Allen, shaking as with palsy, "I—I—I am—I am innocent. I—I swear—I'm innocent!"

CHAPTER XIV

WHAT DR. SCOTT SAW

Dora made no reply. In spite of his asseverations of innocence, she saw that he felt himself in a trap. His pallid face, his wild eyes, his trembling hands—all these signs hinted at a realization of his helpless position. Week by week since that fatal conversation he had grown thinner and more haggard. He was the shadow of the comely lover who had met her by the wayside when she had taken him to see Edermont. He looked round the room, as though searching for some means of escape. One would have thought that the officers of the law were already at the door, and that he was guilty. Dora knew that this was not the case, but could not be sure until she heard his explanation. Suddenly he threw up his hands with a gesture of despair.

"I was mad on that night," he said in a hoarse tone.

Dora drew back with a gasp. Was he about to confess to the crime and allege temporary insanity by way of excuse? A violent trembling seized all her limbs, and she was obliged to lean against the table while waiting for his next words.

"You say Joad saw me?" he asked, looking at her. "Joad can denounce me?"

"No," she murmured, "he will not denounce you."

"But why should he show me such mercy?" cried Allen with haggard surprise. "He admires you; he is jealous of me. To get rid of me he would willingly place a noose round my neck."

"That is true, Allen. But—you are safe from him. He—he has asked me to be his wife."

"Ah!" said he, jealously seizing her hands. "And you—you—— No!" He abruptly tossed her hands away. "You could never bring yourself to marry that wretch, even for fifty thousand pounds."

"He does not wish for that money," said Dora, with a calmness which surprised herself; "he wants me."

"Like his insolence! Of course you told him that such a thing was impossible!"

Dora raised her eyes to his with a look of pain.

"How could I?" she said slowly. "He saw you at the Red House on that night."

"Dora"—Allen again seized her hands—"you are sacrificing yourself to save me?"

"I can do no less, Allen. I love you. Ah!" she cried, with a burst of tears, "you will never know how I love you. I have suffered from your cruelty, your desertion, from your strange silence, but I still love you, as I have always done. As I cannot be your wife and make you happy, I can still marry this man and save you from the consequences of your crime."

"Dora! You do not believe that I am guilty?"

"No, Allen, no; still, I cannot understand. You have refused me your confidence; you say you were mad on that night. Morally speaking, you are innocent, I am certain. But still, in a moment of anger——"

"I swear that I did not touch him!" cried Allen violently. "I admit that I was at the Red House on that night. He asked me to come."

"I guessed that. Joad posted a letter to you."

"Yes, yes. Wait!" He ran into the next room, wherein his desk was standing, and in two minutes he returned with a paper. "This is his letter. You see, Edermont asked me to come at midnight to the Red House—to enter by the postern gate, which he left open for my admittance."

"He wished to add something to the conversation of the week before," said Dora, reading the letter. "But, my poor Allen, this letter rather condemns than saves you. It shows conclusively that you had an appointment at the Red House at midnight. And Mr. Edermont was killed at one o'clock."

"I don't know at what hour he was killed," rejoined Allen, taking back the letter with a gloomy air. "As I told you, I was mad on that night. I lost all idea of time. Whether I was in his study at twelve or one I cannot say, but when I did enter I saw him dead."

"Allen!" Dora uttered a cry of horror. "You saw him dead?"

"He was lying on the floor near the bureau," said Scott, speaking rapidly. "I see him now in my mind's eye—a limp heap, with his white hair dappled with blood. The Zulu club, torn from the savage weapons which decorated the walls, lay near him; his pistol was on the other side. He was dead—dead! Ah God, dead!"

During this recital Dora had sunk into a chair, overcome by the vehemence of his words. Allen strode to and fro, swinging his long arms, with a look of horror on his worn, white face. He pressed his hands to his eyes, as if to shut out the scene which his too vivid fancy had painted. Half swooning, Dora uttered a sob, and the next moment Allen was on his knees beside her, covering her hands with passionate and burning kisses.

"My queen! my saint!" he said hurriedly; "and you would sacrifice yourself for me. You would marry this drunkard, this parasite, this vile reptile, to save me from danger! No, Dora. No, I have been weak and foolish, but I am not guilty—I swear that I am not guilty. You shall not shield me at the cost of your own ruin. Oh, if I could only tell you all! But I dare not, I dare not!"

Carried away by his passion, angered at the sense of his weakness, he could have kissed her feet. But Dora placed her hand on his forehead and reasoned calmly with him. He was not to be saved by giving way to such whirlwinds of passion and despair. The prospect was terrible, but they must both face it boldly. Allen was innocent. He said so, and she believed him. That was everything. If he were not guilty, they might find a way out of the trap into which he had stumbled. To do so, she must know exactly what took place on that fatal night, and to this end she addressed her frenzied lover.

"Allen," she said gravely, "this is not the way to save yourself from arrest, or me from a disgraceful marriage. I have obtained a week's time from Joad to think matters over. In seven days we can do a great deal, and we may see a way out of this terrible situation. Sit down beside me, and tell me exactly what you did on that night."

"I shall not sit down beside you, Dora. I shall remain here at your feet. Ah, Heaven! to think of that cruel bar which prevents our marriage! You should know all, but I have not the courage to tell you."

"Keep silent on that point," said Dora soothingly. "What I want to know now is the story of that night. You returned from London on the second, did you not?"

"Yes," he replied in a tired voice. "In that conversation I had with Edermont he made certain statements which I could not believe. He said I could verify them in London, and told me how and where I could do so. I could not rest until I knew the truth, therefore I caught the express at Selling and went to town. Alas, alas! I found that he had spoken only too truly, and that you could never be my wife."

Repressing the curiosity which devoured her to learn the terrible secret of which he spoke, Dora smoothed his hair gently, and asked him to relate what had taken place on his return from this mysterious errand. He obeyed her like a child.

"When I came home," he said with thoughtful deliberation, "I found that letter I showed you awaiting me. Edermont asked me to see him in his study at midnight on the second of the month. But how he knew that I should return on that day I cannot guess."

"I can explain," said Dora quietly. "You wrote and told me when you would return, and I showed the letter to my guardian."

"Why did you do that, Dora—especially when you knew about our quarrel?"

"I wished to point out to Mr. Edermont that you had gone to London," replied Dora, "and, if possible, induce him to explain your reason for going there."

"Ah, he knew my reason well enough," said Allen with a frown; "but I suppose he refused to tell you what it was?"

"Naturally. He refused to tell me anything. But now you know how Mr. Edermont learnt the date of your return, and appointed that midnight meeting for the date. Go on, Allen."

"I was pleased to get his invitation," continued Allen, picking up the thread of his story, "as I fancied he might confess something further, likely to ameliorate the distressing situation in which I was placed by his previous revelation. I determined, therefore, to obey the summons, but as it yet wanted three hours till midnight the thought of the delay worked me into a fever of anxiety. The hopes, the fears, the vague terrors which beset me drove me nearly wild. I declare, Dora, that I was like a madman. A hundred ideas came into my head as to how I might do away with the effect of Edermont's secret and regain you. But one and all were dismissed, and I felt more helpless than ever. Only one man could put matters right, and that was the man who put them wrong; so there was nothing left for it but to wait until I saw him at midnight."

"Had you any idea that a third person might be present at your meeting?"

"No. As you see, there is no mention of a third person in the letter, nor did I see a third person in the study—only the dead man's corpse." "Ugh!"—Allen shuddered—"I shall never forget that horrible sight."

"It was gruesome enough in the morning," said Dora with a shiver, "so it must have been doubly horrifying at night. Well, did you remain indoors until you went to the Red House?"

"No. I could not rest; I could not bear the confinement. I felt that I must be up and doing, so, in sheer despair, I went out on my bicycle. Where I went I do not know. The night was as bright as day with the rays of the moon, and I had sufficient sense to guide the machine rightly, while running blindly along, not knowing or caring whither I was going. I went up hill and down dale along those weary roads, until I wore myself out. Physically exhausted, for I must have been riding at nearly top speed for hours, I turned in the direction of Chillum. At what time I got there I do not know."

"You had your watch with you?"

"Yes; but in my then perturbed state of mind it never struck me to look at it."

"Mr. Joad said he saw you pass his cottage shortly before twelve o'clock."

"It might have been," said Allen indifferently; "but to my mind it was nearer one o'clock. Indeed, it must have been, for, according to your showing, the murder was committed about that time, and when I entered the study I found Edermont dead."

"Dead! Poor soul!" cried Dora, clasping her hands.

"The postern-gate was open," continued Allen rapidly, "also the side-door of that deserted drawing-room. This did not surprise me, as I had been led to expect from the letter that the way would be clear for me to enter. When I went into the study I was struck with horror at the sight. A candle, wasted nearly to the socket, was burning on the bureau. The desk itself was hacked and smashed, and the drawers forced open, as you saw it in the morning. Hundreds of letters and papers were scattered about, some on the bureau itself, others on the floor, and in the midst of all this disorder lay the ghastly dead body, terrible to look at in the pale glimmer of the expiring candle. The pistol was on one side, the knobkerrie on the other, and the dead man, with his face and head beaten and disfigured, lay between."

"Did you hear anyone, or see anyone?"

"I heard nothing, I saw nothing. The door leading to the hall was closed, and there was no sign of the assassin. I saw in a flash the terrible position in which I was placed. I had quarrelled with Edermont, and here I was, in his private room at midnight, standing beside his dead body. I might be accused of the murder, and condemned on circumstantial evidence—for, on the face of it, I could make no defence. As I looked with horror on the scene, with these thoughts in my mind, the candle flamed up in one expiring flash, then died out in a blue flicker. I was alone in the darkness with the dead man; and, seized with a sudden panic—surely excusable under the circumstances—I turned and fled rapidly. In two minutes I was on my bicycle, running full speed for Canterbury. That is all I know, Dora."

Dora considered for a few moments after he had finished.

"You are sure that there was nobody else in the Red House on that night?" she asked, after a pause.

Allen hesitated.

"I did not intend to speak," he murmured; "but for my own sake I must tell you all. When I was coming into Chillum I met a woman going towards Canterbury on a bicycle."

"A woman, Allen! And at midnight—alone! Who was she?"

"At the time I passed her I did not know," said the doctor, rising; "but on my return journey, when I had left the house after the murder, I met her again, by the railway bridge. She was wheeling her machine down the hill, and called out to me to help her. The tyre of her back wheel was punctured. I got off at once, notwithstanding my anxiety to get home, and, with the aid of guttapercha, I soon mended the tiny hole. Then we rode on together until our roads parted."

"Do you know who she was?" asked Dora for a second time.

"Yes," said Allen quietly. "I recognised her at once." He produced a brooch from his waistcoat pocket. "I found this in Edermont's study, where it had no doubt been dropped by her."

"How do you know?"

"By putting two and two together. Look at the brooch."

Dora did so. It was a slender bar of pale gold, to which two letters formed of small pearls were attached. She uttered an exclamation of astonishment as she read them out. "L.B.," she said; "that stands for——"

"For Laura Burville," finished Allen quickly. "Exactly. Laura Burville was the woman I met coming from Chillum. And, by the evidence of the brooch, Laura Burville was the woman who was in Edermont's study on the midnight of the second of August."

CHAPTER XV

THE PEARL BROOCH

So the long-expected had happened at last, and the inevitable woman appeared on the scene. Dora was hardly astonished to hear of Lady Burville's connection with the crime. She had always believed that, sooner or later, the name of this woman would come into the matter. Nevertheless, it was terrible that she should have killed the wretched man with whom, in some mysterious fashion, she had been associated twenty years before. With the pearl-lettered brooch in her hand, Dora considered the position in which she was placed, the discovery she had made.

"Do you think that Lady Burville really did kill him, Allen?" she asked in a hesitating voice.

"Who can say?" answered Scott wearily. "I should be loath to accuse her on insufficient evidence. But look at the matter as it stands. Lady Burville fainted at the sight of Edermont; she asked me questions as to his whereabouts. On the night of the murder she visits him, as is proved by the finding of that brooch in the study. Immediately after passing her on the road I enter the house, to find Edermont dead. So far as we know, no one else was in the house on that night; so the inference must be drawn that this woman murdered your guardian. Yes," said Allen thoughtfully, "I think there is a strong case to be made out against Lady Burville."

"But her motive, Allen?" expostulated Dora. "She would not commit so terrible a crime without a motive."

"I cannot guess her motive, Dora. I am as ignorant of Lady Burville's connection with the dead man as—as—you are."

"But, Allen," said Dora, hesitating, "was not her name mentioned by Mr. Edermont during that conversation?"

"Yes. He asked me where she was staying, but he gave me no information about her. She has nothing to do with the bar to our marriage. At least, I do not think so."

"Then you are not certain?"

"No," said Allen in a low voice; "I cannot say that I am certain."

Dora looked at him impatiently, and a sigh escaped her. Evidently he was determined to give her no clue to the unravelling of these enigmas, and what she discovered she would discover unaided. Nevertheless, she did not lose heart, but took up the burden which he had laid down.

"Why did you not tell me this before, Allen?"

"How could I?" he said vehemently. "By visiting the Red House on that night I was in a dangerous position. If my movements had been known, I might have not only lost what little practice I have, but have been in danger of arrest. Even now I may be called upon to exonerate myself should this man Joad speak."

"Joad will not speak," said Dora quietly; "at all events, not for a week. As I said before, a great deal may be done in seven days. You must let me take away this brooch."

Allen looked at her with an air of astonishment.

"Why do you wish to take away the brooch?" he asked.

"I'll answer that question later on. Lady Burville is not now at Hernwood Hall?"

"I believe not," replied Scott. "She returned to London, I think, shortly after the discovery of the murder of Edermont. To my mind, her sudden departure seems suspicious."

"On the face of it, I agree with you that it does," assented Dora. "But from what I have heard of the medical evidence, I doubt if Lady Burville killed Edermont—the murder was so brutal."

"You are right there. The assassin must have had brutal instincts and a strong physique. Now, Lady Burville is small and delicate, not the sort of woman capable of using that heavy knobkerrie, or striking so terrible a blow. But then, Dora," added Allen, with a puzzled air, "if Lady Burville is innocent, who is guilty? There can't have been anyone else in the house on that night."

"Why not? Mr. Edermont wrote letters to other people besides yourself."

"Do you know the names of the persons to whom he wrote?"

"No," replied Dora promptly; "he was careful to post the letters himself."

"But, Dora," expostulated Allen, "why should Edermont convene a meeting of so many people at such a late hour?"

"I cannot guess. The explanation may be contained in the stolen manuscript. All my guardian's actions were wrapped up in mystery, and there may be more people connected with this matter than we dream of. But this is not the point. Can I take away this brooch?"

"As you please," said Allen indifferently; "except to exonerate myself in your eyes, I would not have betrayed Lady Burville, murderess as I believe her to be."

"You would win fifty thousand pounds by doing so."

"Blood money!" said Scott angrily. "No, Dora; I do not wish to build up my fortunes in that way, on the ruin of others. I do not say, should Joad denounce me, that I would keep silent. One must save one's own neck if possible; but otherwise I say nothing, I do nothing. All things thought about, or done, cannot gain me your hand; the rest may go."

"Well, my dear Allen," said Dora, pocketing the brooch, "you refuse to tell me this secret, and I have promised not to press you. But if I can't marry you, at least I can save you."

"By becoming Joad's wife?"

"No; by seeing Lady Burville."

He looked at her in surprise.

"My dear Dora," said he after a pause, "you have no reasonable excuse for seeking an interview with Lady Burville."

"You have just given me an excellent excuse, Allen—the pearl brooch."

"But Lady Burville will know that I have betrayed her."

"No doubt. But I will show her that you have done so to save your own life."

Allen thought.

"What do you intend to do?" he asked abruptly.

"Force Lady Burville to confess her share in these mysteries."

"She will not do that," said Scott, shaking his head. "On the surface she is a frivolous little creature, but from what I saw of her I am inclined to believe that such frivolity conceals a strong will."

"No doubt, Allen. She must be a clever and merciless woman to plan and carry out so dexterous a crime. I do not see why you should save her life at the expense of your own. Leave me to deal with her, and I'll force her to speak."

"Would you have her arrested for the crime?"

"If Joad denounces you, I shall denounce her," said Dora quietly; "but there may be no necessity for such an extreme course. Wait until I see her."

"But you do not know where to find her."

"Oh, I can get her address from her late host, Sir Harry Hernwood."

And with this decision Dora took her leave. Here one may pause to reflect on the difference between these characters—a difference accentuated the more by the circumstances in which they found themselves entangled. It cannot be denied that Dora bore herself the better of the two. Shrewd, cool and determined, she saw her way to a definite end, and strove steadily towards its attainment. Allen, on the other hand, was dilatory and wavering. Knowing of a bar to his marriage, he should have informed the girl what this bar was, and have left her to judge of its insuperability. But this is exactly what he shrank from doing. He preferred to wait the turn of events, to refrain from action, until it was forced upon him. No; Allen Scott was not an heroic character. Dora knew this, despite her preference for him above all other men. Indeed, as is the way with good women, she loved him all the better for such weakness. However, as matters now were arranged, Allen sulked like a modern Achilles in his tent, and Dora went forth to take action.

With characteristic decision, she had determined upon her future course. To get the address of Lady Burville from Sir Harry, to call on Lady Burville in town, and to learn all she could of the events of the night from Lady Burville before leaving her house—this was the programme sketched out and adhered to by Dora Carew. As a first step towards the accomplishment of her purpose, she turned off the main road and took that which led to Hernwood Hall. She reached it before half-past six—an awkward hour for a call—and on inquiring for Sir Harry she was shown into the drawing-room. Here she was saluted by the man she came to see, and to whom she apologized for the lateness of her visit.

"You must excuse me, Sir Harry," said Dora calmly. "I am Miss Carew, of the Red House, and I leave for London to-morrow by an early train. Hence my calling on you at so late an hour. If you would be so kind as to give me the address of Lady Burville, I should esteem it a favour."

This abrupt speech was hardly a graceful one under the circumstances; but Dora was so taken up with the intrigue in which she found herself involved that she paid no attention to necessary social observances. Sir Harry, a dapper little man, mincing and polite, was not at all indisposed to grant this request, especially to so handsome a woman.

"Charmed to oblige you, Miss Carew," said he in a gallant fashion; "but—you will pardon me—may I ask why you wish for this address?"

"Certainly," replied Dora, prepared for the question; "I have picked up a pearl brooch on the road"—she was afraid to state the actual finding-place—"which I have reason to believe belongs to Lady Burville. I wish to return it to her in person."

"May I see the brooch, Miss Carew?"

"Certainly."

She handed it to him in silence. Sir Harry examined it, noted the initials, and returned it with a polite bow and the required information.

"The address of Lady Burville," said he amiably, "is No. 22, Jersey Place, Mayfair. I am sure she will be greatly obliged to you for returning her brooch, which I recognise as one she usually wore. No doubt she dropped it on the road when out on her bicycle. But if it would save you trouble, Miss Carew, I should be happy to forward it myself."

"There is no necessity, thank you," replied Dora, rising to take her leave. "I am going up to town to-morrow, in any event, so I can easily return it myself. Good evening, Sir Harry. I thank you for your good nature in seeing me at this hour, and your kindness in giving me the address."

"Pray do not mention it, my dear Miss Carew. I am delighted to be of service to you."

During this conversation Sir Harry had discreetly refrained from remarking on the tragic end of Julian Edermont. He knew that Miss Carew was the ward of the dead man; but, afraid of a scene, and detesting trouble, he judged it wiser to ignore the fact. In the same way he gave the address of Lady Burville at once, as he was anxious to rid himself of his visitor. Sir Harry Hernwood, in a word, was a fool; and for that reason Dora was successful in her mission. A wiser man would have withheld the address of his late guest until better assured of the errand of the inquirer.

Dora thought of all these things as she rode homewards, and congratulated herself that Sir Harry had proved so foolish and weak. She had the address of Lady Burville, and could obtain the interview she sought. Now it remained to force the woman into confession of the crime by means of the pearl brooch. It would be difficult for Lady Burville to explain its presence in the study without inculpating herself in the murder.

"Mrs. Tice," said Dora that night when Joad had departed, "I am going to town to-morrow."

"Very good, Miss Carew," said the housekeeper placidly. "Will you return in the evening?"

"Probably. If I do not, I shall send you a wire. But I want you to conceal from Mr. Joad that I have gone to London."

"I shall not tell him, Miss Carew, if you do not wish him to know. But why, if I may be so bold?"

"Oh," said Dora, with a peculiar look, "I'll tell you that when I return."

"You will tell me on your return?" repeated Mrs. Tice, looking shrewdly at her companion. "I hope nothing is wrong, miss?"

"Everything is wrong. I am endeavouring to put everything right."

"That will be difficult, my dear young lady, in your present state of ignorance. You do not know all."

Dora laughed.

"I know more than you give me credit for, Mrs. Tice. Allen has told me something."

The ruddy face of the housekeeper blanched suddenly.

"Not—not—the secret?" she stammered.

"Not the secret you know of," replied Dora. "I am still ignorant of the bar to our marriage."

"Then what has Mr. Allen told you?" asked Mrs. Tice, reassured on this point.

"Ah, that's my secret. If you will not confide in me, I do not see why I should confide in you."

"Mr. Allen could have said nothing very dreadful," was Mrs. Tice's reply; "we had a talk together on the evening he returned from London, and he told me everything then."

"No doubt," said Dora, who was pleased to stimulate the housekeeper's curiosity, "but he did not tell you some things, for the simple reason that 'some things' had not happened. Remember, Mrs. Tice, the night of Allen's return was the night of the murder."

"The murder!" repeated Mrs. Tice in a scared tone.

"Yes. Allen did not tell you what he knew about that," said Dora, and left the room.

CHAPTER XVI

DORA IS STARTLED

The next day Dora excused her absence to Joad on the plea of a visit to a friend living the other side of Canterbury, and stated furthermore that she would not return until late that evening. It was absolutely necessary to make some such statement, as she knew not what conclusion would be drawn by the old man did he learn that her true destination was London. She suspected him of knowing more of Lady Burville than he chose to confess; and, with such knowledge, he might guess her intention. If so, it might be that he would warn Lady Burville, did he know her address, which was by no means unlikely; therefore Dora was resolved to keep him in ignorance of her plan. To blind Joad was no easy task, as he was artful, dangerous, and—she more than suspected—merciless.

To avert all suspicion, she rode to Selling on her bicycle, and there caught the early train to London. Resolved on economy, she purchased a third-class ticket, and had just time to stumble into a carriage before the train started. Then she became aware that she had but one companion in the compartment—a man. He turned his head as the train began to move, and she saw with astonishment and some annoyance that it was Mr. Pride. "Never mind," she thought, returning his greeting with a stiff nod; "he can tell Joad on his return if he pleases. It will then be too late for the old man to do anything, as I shall have seen Lady Burville."

Like Joad, this man was another protégé of Edermont's, who had procured for him a small post in a private school at Chillum. Pride was not unlike his late patron, being short and insignificant-looking, with a white beard, hardly so luxuriant as that of Edermont, and silvery-white hair. In the distance the resemblance was striking, but a closer inspection showed the difference between the two men, as Pride was plump and rosy, with mild eyes and a good-natured smile. He rubbed one fat hand over the over, and saluted Miss Carew in his usual cheery fashion.

"I am glad to see you looking so well, Miss Carew," he said brightly. "You go to London?"

"Only for the day, Mr. Pride," replied Dora coldly.

"Ah! no doubt you wish to get away from those pests who swarm round the Red House in the hope of gaining a fortune."

"Those amateur detectives?" said Dora quietly; "do you think they will discover the truth?"

"Who knows?" was Pride's reply; "they will do their best to do so. Fifty thousand pounds is worth the earning."

Dora considered for a moment, then turned on him suddenly.

"You were at Canterbury on the night the murder was committed?"

"Till close on eleven," returned Pride easily; "then I walked back to Chillum."

"And you went into Mr. Joad's house?"

"I did. I was with him at one o'clock."

"Did you meet anyone on a bicycle as you walked to Chillum from Canterbury?"

"Why," replied the schoolmaster after a moment's pause, "I met two people, and each rode a bicycle. One, a man, was riding towards Chillum; the other, a woman, was making for Canterbury."

"Did you know who they were?"

"I, my dear Miss Carew!" said Pride in great surprise—"why, no. I took no particular notice of them, in the first place; and in the second, they flitted along so swiftly and noiselessly that I was hardly aware of their passing."

"I suppose you have no clue to the assassin?" said Dora abruptly.

"No. If I had, I should not scruple to earn the fortune."

"Can you conjecture the motive for the crime, Mr. Pride?"

"I—am—afraid—not," said Pride slowly. "I knew Mr. Edermont well; but there was nothing in his past life likely to endanger his safety."

"He thought otherwise. Mr. Edermont was always haunted by the dread of a violent death."

"I knew that, Miss Carew. Monomania, my dear lady—monomania."

"It could not be monomania if it came true," said Dora impetuously.

"Why not?" replied Pride in an argumentative tone. "Monomania is the dwelling on one particular idea until it fills the thoughts and life of the thinker. Mr. Edermont may have had reason to suppose that his life was in danger; but the original cause may have passed away. Nevertheless, the habit may have continued; and so," added Pride with a shrug, "we may reasonably ascribe our friend's death to a creature of his imagination."

"Your argument is weak," replied Dora spiritedly. "Mr. Edermont believed that he would die a violent death, and what he believed came to pass. That does away with all your sophistries."

"But, Miss Carew, the cause of his fear was done away with before your guardian died."

"How do you know that?"

"Joad told me. We were discussing the possibility of the existence of this unknown enemy whom Mr. Edermont feared; and Joad mentioned that Mr. Pallant had set that fear at rest."

"Do you mean to say that Mr. Pallant told him his enemy was dead?"

"Joad thought that such was the case."

"Then you must see," cried Dora triumphantly, "that such a supposition does away with your theory of monomania. Evidently Mr. Edermont's fear was founded on no fancy, but on fact."

"Well, I will agree with you for the sake of argument;" said Pride hastily; "but granted that all you say is true, it brings us no nearer the solution of the mystery. Admitting that the enemy whom Mr. Edermont feared really existed: if such enemy died, as we suppose Mr. Pallant told our poor friend, who killed him, and verified his lifelong prediction that he would come to a violent end?"

"I understand your meaning," was Dora's reply; "but I do not think all the talking in the world will aid us to discover the actual assassin. What is your belief, Mr. Pride?"

"I cannot say that I have any particular belief, Miss Carew. These criminal problems are too intricate for me."

"Don't you wish to earn the reward?"

"I should not mind doing so," replied Pride, with a good-natured laugh. "No man in his senses would lose the chance of gaining fifty thousand pounds. All the same, I am not clever enough to win it. I do not see where to begin."

"Do you think that the manuscript in the bureau was the motive for the crime?"

"No. Why should anyone have killed Mr. Edermont to gain a worthless manuscript?"

"It might not have been worthless to the assassin," objected Dora; "it contained the story of Mr. Edermont's past life."

"But what has his past life to do with his violent death?"

"Everything. You forget that Mr. Edermont believed himself to be a threatened man."

"And so we get back to the starting-point of our argument!" laughed Pride.

Dora laughed also; and, finding that they were arguing in a circle, changed that particular line of conversation.

"You knew Mr. Edermont well?" she asked, after a pause.

"Yes—for quite fifteen years. He was very good to me, and helped me to the post I now hold."

"Did you know Mr. Edermont at Christchurch?"

"Christchurch?" repeated Pride slowly. "No; I did not know him then. Did he live there?"

"I believe so," said Dora curtly, and closed the conversation.

Evidently there was nothing to be learnt from Pride. His knowledge of Edermont only extended back fifteen years; and Dora believed that the motive of the crime was to be found as far back as twenty. Moreover, if he knew anything conclusive, he would be certain to utilize it for his own benefit, and thus gain the reward. Under these circumstances Dora hardly regarded Pride in the light of an important factor in the course she was pursuing, and took no further notice of him from that point of view. They chatted on indifferent subjects until the train arrived at Victoria Station. Here Pride took his leave, and Dora went forward on her mission.

Jersey Place was easily found by asking a convenient policeman. Dora was impressed with the magnificence of the houses and by the aristocratic seclusion of the square. If possible, No. 22 was even more imposing than the surrounding mansions, and as Dora rang the bell she could not help thinking that she was undertaking a difficult task. Here was a rich and titled lady, evidently a power in society, fenced round, as it were, by wealth and position. Yet she proposed to accuse this powerful personage of a crime; she intended to save her lover at the cost of casting down this formidable goddess from her pedestal. It was a dangerous, almost a hopeless, task, but Dora did not shrink from its fulfilment. Too much depended upon the issue of the coming interview for her to retreat at the eleventh hour.

She was introduced by the footman into a small anteroom on the left of the entrance-hall, and there she remained while he took her card up to Lady Burville. In a few moments he returned with the information that his mistress would see her. Dora followed the man upstairs, and was shown into the drawing-room. It was empty at the moment, and she had ample leisure to survey the splendid room, and its still more splendid furniture. The apartment was sumptuous in the extreme. Everything that art and luxury could supply was gathered together between these four walls. The East and the West had contributed to adorn this house. It was more like a palace than the residence of a private person, and gave Dora large ideas of the wealth of Sir John Burville.

His portrait—as she guessed—hung in a conspicuous part of the room. A strong, burly man he appeared to be, with a shrewd, coarse face. Parvenu was writ large on his whole personality, and Dora could guess from his lowering looks that he possessed a violent temper. The portrait was not prepossessing, and she left it to look at the picture of a frail and delicate woman. This, without doubt, was Lady Burville, and her suspicion was confirmed in a few minutes, for as she was contemplating the portrait the door opened to admit the original.

Lady Burville was small, slender, and usually as daintily tinted as a statuette of Dresden china. But at the present moment her face was pale, and her eyes, filled with alarm, looked apprehensively at Dora from under the loose fringe of her golden hair. Arrayed in a tea-gown of some white filmy material, she looked like a ghost as she glided towards the girl. Dora put these terrified looks down to a secret knowledge of her guilt, and believed in her own mind that Lady Burville had really slain Mr. Edermont. But again, she thought, it was impossible that so frail a creature could have struck so deadly a blow. Yet, why was she so terrified?

"Miss Carew, I believe?" said Lady Burville, trying to smile with white lips. "Will you not be seated?"

"No, thank you, Lady Burville," replied Dora stiffly. "I am obliged to you for granting me this interview."

"I am only too pleased. You are a ward of Mr. Edermont's, I believe?"

"I was his ward, Lady Burville."

"Yes, yes; how stupid of me! I forgot about that terrible murder."

Dora deliberately produced the pearl brooch from her pocket, and held it out towards the other.

"Perhaps this will refresh your memory?" she said slowly.

"My brooch!" said Lady Burville in surprise. "How did you come by it? How did you find it?"

"I did not find it, but Dr. Scott did."

"Really! Where?"

"On the floor of the room in which Mr. Edermont was killed."

Lady Burville's face turned even whiter than it was before.

"I—I do not understand," she stammered, shrinking back.

"I can explain," continued Dora pitilessly. "You visited the Red House on the night of the second of August; you dropped this brooch there, and you there killed my guardian."

"No, no! I—I did not! Who dares to say such a thing?"

"I dare," said Dora calmly. "I say it again. You killed Mr. Edermont."

"What—what proof have you?" gasped Lady Burville, seizing a chair to keep herself from falling.

"The proof of this brooch; the evidence of Dr. Scott, who met you returning from the Red House. You need not deny it, Lady Burville. I believe you to be guilty, and I shall denounce you."

"No, no! You cannot—you dare not!"

"Why?"

Lady Burville fell at her feet in a passion of tears.

"I am your mother," she cried, "your unhappy mother!"

CHAPTER XVII

A STORY OF THE PAST

"My mother!" Echoing Lady Burville's exclamation, Dora stepped backward and surveyed with amazement the weeping woman kneeling at her feet. The situation perplexed her. She could not believe that Lady Burville spoke truly in claiming so close a relationship, and deemed that it was some trick to avert the danger of being arrested for the crime. She frowned as this thought came into her mind, and turned away coldly.

"I do not believe you, Lady Burville. My parents are dead."

"Your father is dead," said Lady Burville, rising slowly, "but your mother lives; I am really and truly your mother. Why should I say what is not true?"

"Oh, you have enough excuse to do so," said Dora quietly. "You hope to close my mouth, and escape the consequences of your crime."

"My crime! You believe, then, that I killed Mr. Edermont?"

"I do. You were in the room alone with him, and left the house hurriedly. When Dr. Scott was coming from Canterbury he met you."

"He met me twice," said Lady Burville calmly; "once when I was coming from Chillum, and again when he assisted me to repair my bicycle."

"Then you do not deny that you were at the Red House?"

"No; I can hardly do so in the face of the discovery of the pearl brooch. It is mine; I thought I had lost it on the road, but as it was found in Mr. Edermont's study I admit that I was there on the night of the second of August. If I were guilty, I would not admit as much, even to my own daughter."

"I am not your daughter. Give me some proof that you are my mother."

"What proof do you want?" asked Lady Burville helplessly. "You cannot alter existing facts. If you choose to listen, I can tell you so much of my history as may convince you that what I say is true."

She seated herself on a near sofa, and put a frivolous lace handkerchief to her eyes. Dora looked at this woman, so frail, so helpless, so devoid of brain and courage, and pity entered her soul. If this was indeed her mother, the relationship was nothing to be proud of. And yet, would she confess to such a thing if it were not true? Dora could not answer this question, and resolved to suspend her judgment until she had heard the promised history. With some pity she seated herself beside the feeble little woman.

"I am willing to hear your story," she said kindly; "but first you must assure me of your innocence."

"Innocence! Oh, as to the murder. Yes, I am innocent. I never touched Julian; I did not kill him. I would not kill a fly. Who says I am guilty?"

"Dr. Scott saw——"

"I know he saw me!" interrupted Lady Burville impatiently. "I do not deny it. But did he see the dead body of Mr. Edermont, since he is so sure of my guilt?"

"He found your brooch lying by the dead body."

"Ah! And what was he doing at the Red House on that night? When I left Julian, he was alive and well. No doubt Dr. Scott killed him, and blames me for the crime."

"I do not believe that," said Dora decidedly. "Allen is innocent."

"You think so because you love him," said Lady Burville bitterly. "No doubt you are right, my dear; but if he is innocent, who is guilty? Not I—not—— Don't look at me like that, Dora. I swear I did not kill Julian. How dare you accuse your mother of such a horrible thing!"

"You forget I am not yet prepared to accept you as my mother."

"I do not see why you should," said Lady Burville quietly. "I have not acted the part of a mother towards you. But what could I do? Julian took you away from me when you were a year old."

"Had Mr. Edermont the right to do so?"

"Yes. He was my husband!"

"Your husband!" cried Dora in astonishment. "Do you mean to say that Mr. Edermont was my father?"

"I say nothing of the sort," retorted Lady Burville impatiently. "Julian was my second husband; you were the offspring of my first."

"Then my father is dead?"

"No, he isn't; I am sure I don't know; I thought he was, but it seems he isn't," said Lady Burville incoherently. "Oh dear, oh dear! what a tangle it all is!"

"I cannot understand," said Dora in perplexity. "Perhaps if you tell me your story from the beginning I may gather what you mean."

"I shall tell you as much as suits me," replied Lady Burville, "but I cannot tell you all. It is too terrible!" She shuddered, and looked round. "Perhaps you may be able to help me, Dora; I am in the power of a man."

"Of what man?"

"Of Augustus Pallant. You know, he was down at Hernwood with me. Oh, my dear, he is a terrible man, and he knows all."

"Knows all what?"

"All my story—all your story—all Julian's story. He threatened to tell my husband." Here her eyes wandered to the stern-faced portrait. "I am so afraid of my husband," she said, with a burst of tears, "and Mr. Pallant is merciless. Oh, my dear, my dear, if you could only help me!"

"Tell me your story, and I may be able to do so," said Dora cheerfully.

She was beginning to believe that Lady Burville spoke truly, and that she was really her mother. It seemed doubtful as to whether she was guiltless or guilty, and Dora was prepared to hear both sides of the question before judging. But even if Lady Burville proved the truth of her assertion, Dora was not prepared to take her for a parent, and be sentimental over the discovery. Mother and daughter had been so long parted and estranged, that no revival of the maternal or filial feeling was possible. Dora pitied her mother; she was sorry for her; but she did not love her. In the meantime Lady Burville told her story, in her usual flippant manner, with many tears. The woman's nature was shallow in the extreme.

"I was married to your father at an early age," she said. "He was a sea captain, and immediately after the honeymoon he went to sea. I lived at Christchurch, in Hants, while he was away. Mr. Edermont was there also."

"Is not Edermont a feigned name?" asked Dora suddenly.

"How clever you are!" said her mother. "Yes; Mr. Edermont's real name was Dargill—Julian Dargill. He was an old admirer of mine, and wanted to marry me, but I was forced by my parents to become the wife of George Carew."

"Then I am really and truly Dora Carew?"

"Of course—your father's name. Well, after a few months I received news that my husband's ship was lost off the coast of Africa. All hands were drowned except the first mate. He was saved, and brought the story to England. So you see, my dear, I was a widow six months after marriage."

"Are you sure that my father was drowned?" demanded Dora doubtfully.

"I am coming to that," said Lady Burville impatiently. "He was said to be drowned; and after a year of mourning I married Dargill."

"You married Julian Edermont?"

"Yes; what else could I do? I was comparatively poor; I had no friends to speak of. Dargill was rich, so I married him. We were quite happy, he and I, and he was very fond of you, my dear."

"Oh! I was born then?" said Dora, rather naïvely, it must be confessed.

"Certainly. Don't I tell you I married Dargill a year after your father died—eighteen months after my first marriage? Well, we were happy; and then your father returned. He also had been saved by some natives, who detained him on the Gold Coast. He managed to escape, and returned to England. Of course, he sought me out at Christchurch; and then, my dear," added Lady Burville impressively, "there was trouble."

"Between my father and Mr. Dargill, alias Edermont?"

"Yes. Dargill was away at the time, and they never met. He was a coward, you know, my dear, and afraid of your father's violent temper—and he had a violent temper, truly awful. Dargill fled to America. George Carew followed him. Then Dargill escaped him in San Francisco, and returned to England. He wrote to me from London, and offered me an annuity if I would let him take you away."

"And you did," said Dora reproachfully.

"What could I do?" said her mother fretfully. "I was poor without Dargill's money. I could hardly keep you alive, and Carew had left me in his search for Dargill. I accepted the annuity and let you go. Then Dargill disappeared, and I never heard of him again till I saw him in Chillum Church."

"Did you make no attempt to find him?" asked Dora coldly.

"No; why should I have done so?" said Lady Burville. "He was not my real husband, you know, since my first—your father, my dear—was alive. I never wanted to set eyes on Dargill again. I am sure he got me into enough trouble as it was. He absolutely worried me into marrying him, and, as he was rich, I thought it best to do so. We should have been happy enough if Captain Carew had not proved to be alive. Then I wished I hadn't married Dargill."

"Because you loved my father so?"

"No, it wasn't that exactly," babbled Lady Burville, with great simplicity. "But Carew had a dreadful temper, and I thought he might kill me. However, he was more angry at Dargill than at me, and if he had caught him I really believe he would have killed him. But Dargill got away; he was an artful little creature, but a frightful coward. I don't know how I ever came to marry such a mouse of a man."

"You forget he was rich."

Dora could not forbear making this satirical remark. Every word that came out of Lady Burville's mouth showed her to be a vain, shallow fool; a heartless woman, who cared more for dress and gaiety and money than anything else. On the whole, Dora thought it was just as well that Dargill, alias Edermont, had taken her away. She never would have got on with so frivolous a parent as Lady Burville.

"You are right; he was rich," said her mother artlessly. "I married him for his money, and never saw him after he left me for at least twenty years. I did not mind much. But I did get a shock when I saw him in Chillum Church. I recognised him at once, in spite of his beard. He had always white hair, you know."

"And that was why you fainted, I suppose?" said Dora bitterly. "No doubt you are my mother, but you have acted anything but a mother's part towards your child."

Lady Burville whimpered, and tried to take Dora's hand. The girl drew away coldly. She could not feel any love for this weak little woman, who had acted so despicable a part.

"Go on with your story, Lady Burville," she said calmly. "What of my father?"

"I heard nothing of him for some time, Dora," said her mother, displeased at the lack of affection displayed by her newly-found child. "Then I saw a paragraph in an American paper which said that he was dead. Oh yes! there could be no doubt about it. The name George Theophilus Carew was given in full. It's not a common name, you know. I was satisfied that he was really dead."

"And you married again?"

"What could I do? I was poor," said Lady Burville, for the third time giving her childish excuse. "Yes, I married Sir John Burville. He is a cruel and violent-tempered man, but he has plenty of money, and he is good to me."

"And you are happy?" said Dora, scornful of the weak nature which could draw happiness out of such misery.

"Quite happy—at least, I was—till Augustus Pallant came."

"When did he come? and who is he?"

"He came about two years ago from America. He told me that my husband was not dead, and that I had committed bigamy. I had to pay him to be quiet; he has cost me a lot of money."

"And, knowing this, you still live with a man who is not your husband?"

"Yes; I am not going back to poverty," said her mother defiantly. "I shall remain Lady Burville till I die. Pallant knew all my story. Carew told it to him. He found out that Dargill was living near Canterbury under the name of Edermont. He induced me to go down to Hernwood Hall, and took me to Chillum Church. There I saw Dargill, and fainted. Of course, it was all done on purpose—the brute!"

"Mr. Edermont fainted also," said Dora; "he was afraid."

"I know he was. He was afraid lest Carew should find him out and kill him. He lived in a state of perpetual dread, for he told me so on the night I saw him."

"Why did you go to the Red House at so late an hour?" asked Dora.

"Dargill sent me a note stating that he wanted to see me. I went; what could I do? He might have told Sir John about my past. Oh yes, I went; and Dargill told me that Pallant had been at him for a parcel of letters—an old correspondence between Dargill and myself. Pallant wanted to get them to increase his hold over me and wring money out of me. But Dargill, coward as he was, acted very well. He gave me the letters himself; that was why he sent for me. I went, I got the letters, and I came away. When I left the house Dargill—or Edermont, as he called himself—was as well as you or I."

"But when Allen went into the study after you left it, he found Mr. Edermont dead, and the bureau robbed."

"Then, if Dr. Scott did not kill him, someone else must have done so."

"But Allen had no reason to kill him," argued Dora.

"No," said Lady Burville, "but Carew had."

"My father?"

"Yes; I believe that my first husband killed my second. In a word, George Carew killed Mr. Dargill."

CHAPTER XVIII

PALLANT MAKES A STATEMENT

Dora did not remain long with Lady Burville after she had heard the story; nor did her mother desire her to stay. There was no love lost between them, therefore there was no joy at their meeting, no sorrow at their parting. Lady Burville considered her daughter to be cold, proud, and unsympathetic. Dora saw that Lady Burville was a weak and frivolous fool, whom she could neither respect nor love. They parted with a feeling of mutual relief, but not before Lady Burville had extracted a promise of silence.

"You must say nothing about what I've told you to anybody," she said imploringly. "My husband would never forgive me if he found out my past history. I told it to you so as to clear myself in your eyes as to the murder. Only Pallant knows my story, and he will keep silent while I give him money. As you are my child, you must be silent also. Say nothing—nothing."

"But I wish to find out who killed my guardian," said Dora.

"I tell you it was Carew. No one else had any reason to kill him. If you denounce Carew, you will hang your own father. Promise me to be silent."

"I promise," said Dora curtly, and took her leave in the calmest manner.

She returned to Selling, and thence rode to Chillum on her bicycle. It was close on eight before she got home, and she found Joad waiting for her at the gate. He looked pleased to see her, and wheeled the machine into the grounds.

"You are late," said he, following her every movement with greedy eyes. "I hope you had a pleasant day with your friend."

"Very pleasant, Mr. Joad. Good-night; I am tired."

She walked off with a stiff nod, and left her elderly lover looking after her with a rather sulky expression. He had missed her greatly during the day, and resented her departure when he wanted to have a little chat before retiring to his own domicile across the road.

"Never mind," chuckled Joad, rubbing his hands. "She'll have to marry me, or see Allen Scott in gaol as a murderer. And when we are man and wife, I'll find out some way to tame her proud spirit."

Dora partook of supper with Mrs. Tice, but answered that good lady's questions in a perfunctory manner. The housekeeper was anxious and uneasy. The visit of Dora to town struck her as strange—the more so as she connected it with recent events. Before departing Dora had promised an explanation of her movements, and Mrs. Tice waited for the fulfilment of that promise. But Dora said nothing. She ate her supper, talked on general subjects, and finally took herself off to bed without a word of explanation. Mrs. Tice was annoyed.

"Miss Carew," she said, following her to the door, "I beg your pardon, but you promised to tell me why you went up to town to-day."

"Did I?" said Dora carelessly. "I've changed my mind, then."

"I do not see why you should keep me in the dark, miss," exclaimed the housekeeper, in a mortified tone.

"If you cast back your memory to our last conversation, you will see, Mrs. Tice. You are keeping me in the dark; so, by acting in the same way towards you, I am only giving you a Roland for an Oliver."

"All the same, you could do worse than ask my advice, Miss Carew."

"I have asked it, and you refuse to help me. Now I must see after things in my own way."

"You will get into trouble if you are not careful," said Mrs. Tice sharply.

"It will be no thanks to you if I do not," retorted Dora bitterly. "You have refused to help me."

"What would you have me do, girl?" cried Mrs. Tice, forgetting her respect in her anxiety. "I dare not tell you what I know. Mr. Allen made me promise to be silent."

"Allen is acting in a very foolish manner, and so are you," said Dora quietly; "you seem to think that I am a child, to whom no secret can be confided. In ordinary cases, this would not matter to me, as I am the least curious of women. But as my happiness is at stake, I must strive to learn what you would want concealed."

"It will do you no good if you do find out," said Mrs. Tice sullenly.

"Perhaps not; but at least its discovery will throw a light on the mystery of this murder."

"There you are wrong, Miss Carew. It will do no such thing."

Dora had argued this point before; therefore she made no reply, and with a weary nod prepared to leave the room. Again Mrs. Tice laid a detaining hand upon her sleeve.

"Tell me, my dear," said she timidly, "what is it Mr. Allen said to you about the murder?"

"You had better ask him, Mrs. Tice; it is no good coming to me. Unless you tell me what you know, I shall keep silent as to my knowledge."

"Does Mr. Allen know anything about this crime?"

"Yes, he does; he knows a great deal."

"Does he know who killed Mr. Edermont?"

"He does—and you know also."

"No, no; I—I do not!" gasped Mrs. Tice, shrinking back; "my knowledge has nothing to do with the matter."

"Has your knowledge anything to do with my father?"

Mrs. Tice gasped again, and sank into a chair. For a moment she closed her eyes, and when she opened them again Dora was gone. The housekeeper wiped her face.

"Who can have told her about her father?" she meditated. "If she gets to know about him, there will be trouble."

Then she drank a glass of water, and put away her work. But her thoughts wandered.

"What has come to her?" she said to herself again, as she made all safe for the night. "There is a worried look on her face, an anxious expression in her eyes. And why did she go up to London? Can she have learnt anything about the past? No, no. Mr. Allen knows it, Mr. Joad knows it, and myself. None of the three will tell her. Still, that question about her father! It is very, very strange."

In the meantime Dora was leaning out of her bedroom window, looking into the soft darkness of the night. Overhead the sky was fleecy with clouds, between the rifts of which twinkled the cold stars, and below, between the tree-tops and dry grass, hovered the thick gloom of night. She could see nothing in the shadows; all was as indistinct, as unknown, as strange, as this mystery which was torturing her life.

She had gone seeking, and she had learnt much: that her mother lived, and her father; that the latter had been the incarnation of the deadly fear which had haunted Dargill, alias Edermont, throughout his long life. No wonder he had changed his name, had hidden himself in the Red House, had prayed for deliverance from murder and sudden death, when a man of violent passions had hunted him hot-footed through the world. Dora remembered what a despicable coward the dead man had been, and no longer marvelled at his fears; but what she did wonder at was the change that had come over Edermont after Pallant's visit. Then he had declared that the shadow was lifted from his life; that he could henceforth mix with his fellow-men, and dwell in safety. Such joy could only mean that his enemy was dead. Yet Edermont was dead also, of the very death he feared.

And there was no doubt in Dora's mind that her father had killed him. It seemed a cruel thing, for, after all, in marrying her mother Edermont—or Dargill, as he was called—had sinned unconsciously. Why should her father have so ardently desired his death? Dora began to think that her mother had not told her all, that there was something still hidden—a something which might account for the persistent desire of Carew for the death of Edermont.

Again, she had not asked her mother what was the bar which existed to prevent her marriage with Allen. Dora thought her mother knew this, and might reveal the obstacle. But then she would be forced to tell the portion of her story which she had hidden. Would she do so? Dora was doubtful, for the weak little coquette was as strong as steel in aught that concerned herself. Unblinded by filial love, Dora estimated her mother's character at its true value. There was no further hope of learning the truth in that quarter. And who, then, would tell her—Allen, Joad, Mrs. Tice? She would be forced to ask one of the three to speak. Since she knew so much, she might as well know more. And a fuller knowledge might enable her to save Allen, to marry Allen, to revenge the death of Edermont, and to win the fifty thousand pounds. But yet, all——

"Dreams, dreams; vain, vain dreams!" sighed Dora, and went to bed in as hopeless a frame of mind as can well be imagined.

Fate always arranges matters much better than ourselves. Here was Dora at a dead stop; she knew not what to do, or in which direction to turn. It seemed that no one would advise her as to the future; and that she must be content to lose Allen, and accept the humiliating position of Joad's wife. But while she was steeling her heart to face this dreary prospect Fate was at work, and next morning Pallant appeared. He came to point out the road.

Dora was surprised when Mrs. Tice informed her that a gentleman wished to see her. She was still more surprised when Pallant was shown into the morning-room where she sat. The old supercilious look was on his face, the old cynicism was looking out of his blue eyes, and as he stood bowing, with the strong sunlight glittering on his red beard, he looked as worldly and evil a man as could be imagined. Dora remembered how he had extorted money from her weak mother for over two years, and rose to meet him with a stern face.

"What has brought you here, sir?" she asked coldly.

"You have," said Pallant, calmly taking a seat. "I saw Lady Burville yesterday, and she gave me the gist of your conversation."

"I do not see how it can interest you," said she contemptuously; "you cannot get out of me what I have not got. I am poor, Mr. Pallant."

"More's the pity!" he replied, quite indifferent to her shaft. "With your beauty and my brains, we might do worse than marry!"

"Marry—marry you!"

"I forgot. You are in love with that foolish young doctor," he said in his sleepy voice. "That is a pity. At our first meeting I warned you to beware of Allen Scott."

"I know you did. Why did you warn me?"

"Ah! I see your mother did not tell you everything, Miss Carew, else you would not ask me such a question. I warned you, lest you should give him your heart. It would be foolish to do so, because you can never marry him."

"Why?"

"That is my secret. I don't tell you all I know. It is not worth my while."

Dora looked at him scornfully.

"It is worth your while to blackmail my mother!"

"It pays! it pays!" said Pallant shamelessly. "I must live, you know. Lady Burville is greatly afraid of her present husband, so she keeps me well supplied with money to hold my tongue."

"Where did you learn my mother's history?" said Dora, disgusted with this brutal speech.

"From the best of all authorities—her first husband."

"My father?"

"Your father—George Theophilus Carew. I met him in San Francisco some years ago. He was a drunkard and a gambler, Miss Carew. We had some dealings over cards, for you must know that I am a gambler also, though it is to my credit that I don't drink. One day, in a fit of maudlin fear, he told me his story, and how he was seeking for Julian Dargill."

"Mr. Edermont?"

"Precisely. The man who had taken away his wife. He wanted to kill him."

"To kill him?" echoed Dora, starting; "and—and did—did my father succeed in carrying out his intention? Was it George Carew who killed Mr. Edermont?"

"Not exactly, Miss Carew," responded Pallant dryly, "for the simple reason that before your father could accomplish his object he died himself."

"Died himself! Is my father dead?"

"Dead and buried," said Pallant concisely; "dead and buried."

CHAPTER XIX

MORE MYSTERIES

When Pallant made this remarkable statement he looked up sharply to see how Dora was affected by it. Her face had flushed hotly, and her eyes had brightened. In place of sorrow, her whole expression was that of relief and gladness. Pallant could not forbear a cynical remark on her want of feeling.

"You do not seem sorry to hear that your father is dead, Miss Carew."

"I do not know why I should display a sorrow which I do not feel," she replied quietly. "You must remember, Mr. Pallant, that my parents are nothing to me. I was taken away from them when I was a year old, and I have no feeling of love towards them. I am glad that my father is dead."

"May I ask why?"

"Because, had he lived, he might have been guilty of murder. At least, I am spared the dishonour of having a criminal for a parent."

Pallant chuckled, and seemed about to speak. However, he thought better of it, and merely turned away his face to hide a peculiar smile. Dora took little notice of his action, being absorbed in her own thoughts.

"Is this what you told Mr. Edermont in the conversation you had with him?"

"Yes. I was sorry for the miserable little creature. The thought of Carew roaming the earth in search of him was his constant nightmare. It did not matter to me whether he knew or not. Certainly, it did not affect my plans, so—I never inflict useless cruelty, Miss Carew—I told him the truth: that his lifelong enemy was dead and buried; that henceforward he could sleep in safety."

"The result proved your assertions to be false."

"What is that to me?" said Pallant with a shrug. "I am no prophet, to foretell the day and hour of a man's death. I said that Carew was past harming him. That was true. Carew did not kill him."

"Then who did?"

"My dear young lady, if I could tell you that I should be the richer by fifty thousand pounds; but on that point I am as ignorant as you are. I held your father in my arms when he died; I saw him buried. It was not Carew who killed Dargill, alias Edermont, and there is nothing in the story told to me by your father likely to throw light on the mystery."

"You—you do not think my mother killed him?" faltered Dora.

Pallant scoffed at the idea.

"Could those little hands wield a heavy club? Could those weak muscles deliver so terrible a blow? No, Miss Carew; your mother is too weak, too—if I dare say so—cowardly, to do such a thing. She is as innocent of this death as your father. Dargill's fate is not due to the vendetta of the past."

"It must be due to something of the sort, Mr. Pallant. No one had any interest in killing so harmless a man."

"No one in this neighbourhood, you mean."

"Yes; I have lived here all my life, and I know everything about my guardian. He had few friends, and lived quietly among his books and flowers. Beyond his constant fear lest my father should find him out, I never saw him distressed in any way. And in some things Mr. Edermont was as transparent as a child. If he had been threatened by any person about here, I should have known of it."

"Then you think his death must be due to what took place twenty years ago?"

"Don't you think so yourself, Mr. Pallant?"

"No, Miss Carew, I do not," replied the red-haired man quietly. "If your father had lived I might have held a different opinion. But, knowing the story of the past, you can see for yourself that, excepting Carew, no one had any motive or desire to kill Dargill."

"Then what is your own theory?" asked Dora, rather confounded by this argument.

"Burglary. Yes! Mr. Edermont was known to be rich; this house is in a lonely situation, and I dare say the burglar made himself acquainted with the garrison of the mansion. Two women and one old man—small odds against a sturdy villain. Inspector Jedd, of Canterbury, is also of my opinion. The burglar, or burglars, broke in, ransacked the desk, killed Edermont, who interrupted them, and then bolted. That is my theory, Miss Carew."

"I do not agree with you," replied Dora calmly; "you forget that nothing was taken out of the bureau but that manuscript containing the story of the past."

"How do you know that the manuscript was in the bureau?"

"Mr. Edermont said so in his will."

"Nevertheless, he might have changed its hiding-place," said Pallant coolly, "or my information that his enemy was dead might have induced him to burn it as useless. With the death of Carew ceased all necessity to keep that story in writing. And again, Miss

Carew, how do you know but that money or jewels may have been hidden in the bureau?"

"It is possible, but not probable," replied Dora cautiously; "I don't think Mr. Edermont kept anything there save bills and letters. No doubt he preserved also the packet of letters you wished to obtain."

"And which he gave to Lady Burville," said Pallant. "Very possibly. I was vexed at not getting those letters."

"What information did they contain?"

"Much that I know, and you don't," answered Pallant; "they related to you."

"To me!" cried Dora in surprise. "What about me?"

"Ah!" said Pallant grimly, "that is exactly what I wanted to find out. However, Lady Burville has them now, and she'll keep them."

He made this speech in a tone of such genuine regret that Dora saw he was in earnest. It was no use questioning him upon matters of which he was ignorant, so she changed the subject.

"You warned me once against Allen Scott," said she, after a pause. "Did that mean you believed him to be guilty?"

"No. At the time I made the remark Edermont was alive. Why I warned you was to make you give up the idea of marriage with him. I know from Lady Burville that Scott was here on the night the crime was committed; but for all that I do not believe him to be guilty."

"I am thankful to hear you say so, Mr. Pallant."

"You need not be," replied Pallant coldly. "If I thought Scott was guilty, I should have no hesitation in denouncing him. But I do not see what motive he had to commit so terrible a crime. He could not win you for a wife by doing so; he could not gain a fortune, and he would be running into danger without hope of reward. No; Allen Scott is innocent."

"I believe he is myself," said Dora emphatically; "but you know, Mr. Pallant, he refuses to tell me the secret which Mr. Edermont confided to him, and which prevents our marriage."

"He is quite right to do so, Miss Carew. I know that secret also, and it would do you no good to learn it. Besides, that knowledge had nothing to do with the death of Mr. Edermont."

"But what about the paper taken out of the bureau?"

"If it was not destroyed," said Pallant, "it is hard to say what became of it. The manuscript, as we are told by the will, contained the story of Mr. Edermont's past life. Now, through Carew I know that story, and therefore the contents of that paper. Excepting Carew himself, I know no one who would have killed your guardian for the possession of that written information."

"But undoubtedly the murder was committed to gain possession of the manuscript."

"We don't agree on that point," said Pallant; "but granting for the sake of argument it was so, that is exactly why I can't name the assassin. If the possession of that paper was essential to his safety, if his name was mentioned in it in connection with the past of Mr. Edermont, I am ignorant of some of the past. Evidently Carew did not tell me all."

"It is just as well he did not," said Dora, curling her lip; "you have made bad use of what you do know."

"Oh, a man must live, you know," retorted Pallant coolly, as he rose to take his leave. "I prefer to get money without work, if I can. We all do."

"I'll put a stop to your——"

"Quite right," was the insolent answer, "if you can; but you see, my dear young lady, you can't."

After which remark Pallant bowed himself out of the room. Dora accompanied him as far as the gate, and as he passed through she asked him a question which had been in her mind all the time of the interview. "Why did you come down here?" she asked abruptly. "It was not to condole with me."

"No, it wasn't," candidly admitted Pallant; "but I want fifty thousand pounds, and I thought you might help me to get it."

"I decline to do so," said Dora coldly; "and I don't see how I can help you."

"As you decline to give your aid," said Pallant quietly, "there is no necessity to discuss the matter. But I fancied you might be able to tell me something about Mr. Joad."

"You don't think he killed Edermont?"

"Why not? Certainly I did not know his name in connection with Mr. Edermont's past. But for all that he might have killed his patron."

"For what reason, Mr. Pallant?"

"That is just where I require to be enlightened by you."

"I am afraid I cannot enlighten you," she replied, "and I would not if I could. There is no sense in believing Joad killed my guardian. In the first place, far from being desirable, Mr. Edermont's death was a bad thing to happen for Joad's comfort. In the second, Mr. Joad was in his cottage at one o'clock in the morning, as was proved by Mr. Pride. To my own knowledge, the murder was committed about that time, so Mr. Joad could not have been the assassin."

"It all seems clear enough," said Pallant, preparing to climb into the trap which was waiting for him; "but, all the same, I mistrust

Joad. You say the murder was committed at one o'clock. Joad says he was in his cottage at one o'clock, and calls upon Mr. Pride to substantiate his statement. Very good. We will believe all that. But," added Pallant, gathering up the reins, "your clock in the hall might have been wrong."

After which remark he raised his hat, and drove off smiling. Dora did not think that his remark about the clock was worthy of consideration, for she had set her watch by it before retiring to bed on the night of the second of August. It was right then, and no one could possibly have put it wrong in the meantime. Joad had proved his alibi clearly enough, and there was no possible suspicion that he was guilty of the crime, especially as its committal had not been to his advantage.

Curiously enough, Joad knew nothing of Pallant's visit, nor did Dora intend to inform him of it. He had been in the library all the morning, reading ancient books, and sipping brandy out of the flask he carried constantly in the tail pocket of his dingy coat. Not wishing to disturb him in the midst of his pleasures, Dora returned to her own sitting-room, and sat down to think. While thus employed, Mrs. Tice entered the room with a letter in her hand. She looked distressed.

"My dear young lady," she said hastily, "I am afraid I must return to Mr. Allen. He is ill."

"Ill!" cried Dora, jumping up. "What is the matter with him?"

"I fancy he has fretted himself into a kind of fever," said Mrs. Tice, glancing at the letter. "This has just been sent over. Emma wrote it." Emma was a servant in Scott's house. "Mr. Allen did not want me to be told, but Emma thought it best I should know. I must really return and nurse my dear Mr. Allen," concluded Mrs. Tice, smoothing down her apron with trembling hands.

"You shall go this afternoon," cried Dora. "I'll send Meg to the hotel for a trap, and we will go over together."

Mrs. Tice smiled and looked grateful.

"I hope you won't think me unkind, Miss Carew?"

"Oh dear no! Meg will protect me against Joad," said Dora. And, after a pause, she added abruptly: "You do not ask me what I was doing in London yesterday."

"I did not think you wished to let me know, miss. You refused to tell me last night."

"I know I did; but I'll tell you now, because you may be able to help me. Mrs. Tice," said Dora solemnly, "I have seen Lady Burville."

"Yes, miss; and what of that?" asked Mrs. Tice cheerfully.

"Do you know who Lady Burville is?"

"I know nothing about her, miss, save she's a patient of Mr. Allen's."

"Then I'll tell you, Mrs. Tice: she is my mother."

The housekeeper's ruddy face paled, and she sat down on the nearest chair.

"Your mother, Miss Carew! Are you sure?"

"I am certain. Lady Burville informed me of the relationship, and told me her story."

"In that case," said Mrs. Tice with emphasis, "you know now why a marriage between you and Mr. Allen is impossible."

"That is just what I do not know," was Dora's reply. "My mother did not tell me all her story. Now, I want you to relate what she kept hidden."

"Tell me what you have heard, miss, and I'll see," said Mrs. Tice, after a pause.

"Very good," said Dora, taking a seat near the old dame. "I'll tell my story, you will tell yours, and between us we may save Allen's life."

CHAPTER XX

THE SINS OF THE FATHER

When Dora made that last remark, the face of Mrs. Tice grew red and indignant. She looked at the girl with a fiery eye, and demanded crossly what she meant by saying such a thing. Knowing the attachment of the housekeeper to Allen, this was natural enough.

"The fact is," explained Dora, "Mr. Joad accuses Allen of murdering Mr. Edermont."

"And what next, I wonder!" cried Mrs. Tice in high dudgeon; "it is more likely Mr. Joad killed the man himself! Can he substantiate his accusation?"

"He can state that Allen was in this house on the night of the murder."

"That does not say Mr. Allen committed the crime," retorted Mrs. Tice, her face a shade paler. "Mr. Allen told me in confidence that he had seen the dead body, and had kept silent for his own sake. I quite agreed with him that it was the best thing to do. And he told you also, Miss Carew?"

"Yes, he told me also; but he did not inform Joad."

"Then how does Joad know that Mr. Allen was here on that night?"

"He saw him from the door of his cottage," said Dora quietly; "but you need not be afraid for Allen, Mrs. Tice. I can save him, and close Joad's mouth."

"But how, my dear?" asked the housekeeper, greatly perplexed.

"By becoming the wife of Mr. Joad."

"Mercy on me, Miss Carew! You would not do that!" exclaimed Mrs. Tice, lifting up her hands in horror.

"I won't do it unless I am forced to," said Dora gloomily. "But supposing Joad denounces Allen, how can he defend himself? I know that he is innocent; but his presence here on that night looks guilty."

"Appearances are against him, certainly. But if Mr. Allen is arrested, he will have to save his life by denouncing your father as the murderer."

"My father is not the murderer."

"I say that he is!" cried Mrs. Tice emphatically. "For twenty years George Carew has been hunting down Mr. Dargill—I suppose

Lady Burville told you his real name?—and he caught him at last and killed him."

"You are wrong," said Dora, shaking her head. "I thought as you did before Mr. Pallant arrived. He undeceived me."

"What does Mr. Pallant know about it?"

"He knows everything. He met my father in San Francisco two years ago, and my father told him the whole story before he died."

"Died! Do you mean to say that George Carew is dead?"

"He is dead and buried."

"Captain Carew dead!" muttered Mrs. Tice in a bewildered tone; "dead—and without avenging himself on the man who stole his wife! Then, who killed Mr. Dargill—or rather, Mr. Edermont?"

"I do not know. That is just what I wish to find out."

"No one else had any reason to kill him," said the housekeeper in dismay, "and yet he is dead—dead—murdered. You are right, my dear," she added in a firm tone; "this is a serious matter for Mr. Allen. Joad hates him so that he would willingly perjure himself to see my dear boy hanged. But we must save him, you and I; we must save him, Miss Carew."

"To do so, we must understand one another," said Dora; "you must tell me all."

"I shall do so," cried Mrs. Tice energetically—"yes. Hitherto I have said nothing, out of consideration for your feelings. Now I shall tell you why Captain Carew—your father, my dear—hated Mr. Edermont so deeply. But first let me hear what your mother revealed. I may be able to relate those things which she kept hidden from you."

Thus adjured to confess, Dora related the story of the past, as told to her by Lady Burville—she could not bear even to think of her as "mother." Mrs. Tice listened in severe silence, only nodding her head now and then at some special point in the story. When Dora concluded, she sat quiet for two minutes, then gravely delivered herself of her opinion.

"I see that you do not look upon this woman as a mother, my dear young lady," she said solemnly, "and you are right to do so. May I speak plainly?"

"As plainly as you like, Mrs. Tice. I have no filial feeling for the mother who deserted me, and left her helpless child to be brought up by a stranger."

"Mr. Dargill was scarcely a stranger," corrected Mrs. Tice: "he was your mother's second husband, as she told you. Oh, heavens! you are quite right! Mrs. Carew, as I knew her, was always a light-headed, selfish woman, given over to vanity and pleasure. She cared only for money and idleness, and I'll be bound she was only too glad to get rid of you, so as to give herself a chance of a third marriage as an unencumbered widow. Yet what she came through would have sobered many a woman. But there, Mrs. Carew was always a feeble, frail coquette. She loved only one thing in the world then, and she loves only one thing now—herself."

"Was what she told me true?"

"Oh yes; the tale she told is true enough, but it is trimmed and cut to suit her own ends. She was ashamed to tell you everything, I suppose. A wicked woman she is, Miss Carew, for all that she is your mother. Owing to her coquetry and love of money, poor Mr. Dargill came to his end as surely as if she had killed him herself."

"We don't know that yet," said Dora thoughtfully. "Remember, it was not her first husband who killed him."

"That is true," assented Mrs. Tice. "Nevertheless, I can think of no other person who had an interest in your guardian's death. But I had best tell you my story, Miss Carew, and you can judge for yourself."

"Will your story enable me to discover the real murderer?"

"I don't say that," replied Mrs. Tice reluctantly; "as I said before, you must judge for yourself."

She took her spectacles off and laid them on the table; then, folding her mittened hands on her lap, she began the amended version of that story which Lady Burville had told to Dora. The missing portion, supplied by the memory of the housekeeper, was by far the most exciting episode of the tale.

"The whole affair took place at Christchurch, in Hampshire," she said slowly; "you were right in your guess as to the locality, Miss Carew. I was born and brought up and married there, but twenty-five years ago my husband died, and to support myself I had to go out again to service. Dr. and Mrs. Scott took me in as a nurse to their newly-born child—Mr. Allen, that is. His mother died shortly after giving him birth, and his bringing up was left to me. Dr. Scott took little heed of the child. He was a handsome man, clever in his profession, but fond of going about the country to pleasure parties, and of flirting with his lady patients. He was said to be deeply in love with Mrs. Carew."

"Was my father with her then?"

"No, my dear. This was two years after Mr. Allen was born, and your mother was not married then. A Miss Treherne she was, a pretty, fair-haired girl, shallow and frivolous. She had three suitors: Dr. Scott was one, Mr. Julian Dargill was the second, and Captain Carew the third."

"Was Mr. Edermont rich then?"

"Mr. Julian Dargill was rich," corrected Mrs. Tice. "I prefer to talk of Mr. Edermont by his real name, my dear. He was a weak, effeminate little man, with a noble head, and even then his hair was of a silvery whiteness. It was your description that made me recognise him on the day I showed you his picture."

"He wore no beard then?" said Dora, remembering the portrait.

"No; he was clean shaven. No doubt he afterwards adopted the beard as a disguise to escape Captain Carew. Well, Miss Treherne hesitated between the three suitors for many months. At last her parents decided for her, and for some reason forced her to marry Carew. Why, I do not know, for the Captain was not rich; he was of a violent temper, and usually he was absent at sea. However, she married him and became Mrs. Carew, and shortly after the honeymoon her husband went to sea. While he was absent Mrs. Carew carried on with Mr. Dargill and Dr. Scott. I must say she behaved very badly, and public opinion was quite against her—so much, indeed, that six months afterwards she left Christchurch."

"Had she received news of my father's supposed death then?" said Dora, flushing a little at the disapproving way in which Mrs. Tice spoke of her mother.

"Yes; the mate of Captain Carew's ship was saved, and came home to tell the story. Then Mrs. Carew went away with what small property she had. It was supposed she went to London, and it was noticed that Mr. Dargill left Christchurch after she did. When she reappeared at Christchurch she brought you, Miss Carew, and her new husband, Mr. Dargill."

"That was a year afterwards?"

"Yes, it was quite a year, if not more," said Mrs. Tice. "But she married Mr. Dargill as soon as she could after the report of her first husband's death."

"Was my mother in love with Mr. Dargill?"

"In love!" echoed the housekeeper contemptuously. "She was never in love with anyone but herself."

"Are you not rather hard on her, Mrs. Tice?" said Dora, reflecting that after all this despised woman was her mother, and entitled to some consideration.

"Far from it, my dear young lady," was the emphatic rejoinder of Mrs. Tice; "indeed, out of pity for your position and feelings, I am speaking as well as I can of her. But what can you think of a woman who marries three husbands, and leaves her child to be brought up far away from her? In all these twenty years, Miss Carew," added the old dame, nodding, "I dare swear your mother has not given you a single thought."

"She was willing enough to recognise me," said the girl, attempting a defence of the indefensible.

"She made the best of a bad job, you mean," retorted Mrs. Tice. "If you had not produced that brooch, and showed Lady Burville plainly that she was in your power, she would never have acknowledged the relationship. She knew you could not denounce your own mother, and that is why she spoke up."

"She might wish to make amends for her conduct."

Mrs. Tice shook her head.

"Laura Carew, Laura Dargill, Laura Burville, whatever you like to call her," she said, "is not the kind of woman to regret her conduct in any way. No, no; don't you deceive yourself. Lady Burville was in a trap, and she used her knowledge of your birth to get out of it."

"But all this is beside my question," said Dora, wearied of this constant blame; "I asked you if my mother was in love with Mr. Dargill?"

"No, she was not. What woman could love that miserable little creature? You saw enough of him, Miss Carew, and I am sure you neither loved nor respected him."

"No, I certainly did not," said Dora gravely; "and yet, seeing that he brought me up out of charity, I should certainly have paid him more attention."

"He acted well by you, I don't deny," answered Mrs. Tice reluctantly; "and it was good of him to help Lady Burville by taking charge of you. But what I cannot understand is why he did not stay with her."

"How could he, Mrs. Tice? For, in the first place, his marriage was void, as my father was alive. And in the second, you may be sure that Captain Carew kept a watch on my mother to see if Mr. Dargill would come near her. No doubt he thought to trap him in that way."

"Perhaps," replied Mrs. Tice ambiguously; "but if your father kept watch upon his wife, why did he permit her to marry Sir John Burville?"

"I cannot say," said Dora, colouring; she knew her mother's opinion on that point. "But my mother thought that Captain Carew was dead, else you may be sure that she would not have married again."

"I am not so sure of that," grumbled Mrs. Tice. "Your mother would do anything for money. I remember that she took——"

"Spare me further details," said Dora, blushing, "and finish your story. I have not heard yet why Allen cannot marry me."

"I will say no more, then," said Mrs. Tice hastily; "but, to make a long story short, Captain Carew was not dead, and returned to claim his wife. As I have said, he was madly jealous of his wife, and he had a fearful temper; when he heard that his wife had married again, he swore he would kill her second husband. Dargill was away at the time, and Captain Carew kept such a watch on his wife that she could send no warning. He wished to kill Dargill, who was expected back by a late train. All this came out at the inquest, my dear. It was Dargill's habit to cross the lawn and enter the drawing-room by the French window. As afterwards was stated by the servants, Captain Carew found this out, and hid himself in the drawing-room with a pistol. He saw a man approaching at nine o'clock, and as the stranger stepped into the room he shot him."

"Shot Mr. Dargill?"

"No, Miss Carew," said Mrs. Tice, shaking her head; "he made a mistake. He shot Dr. Scott."

"Dr. Scott—Allen's father!" cried Dora, rising to her feet with a pale face.

"Yes, Mr. Allen's father. Mrs. Dargill, your mother, had sent for him to see how her second husband was to be saved from the fury of Captain Carew. He fell into the trap laid for Mr. Dargill, and was shot through the heart. Then Captain Carew fled, and was never caught. It was supposed that he had gone to the Continent. And now, Miss Carew, you know why Mr. Allen cannot marry you."

"Because—because of that murder!" gasped Dora in broken tones.

"Yes. Mr. Allen cannot marry the daughter of the man who killed his father in cold blood."

CHAPTER XXI

SO NEAR, AND YET SO FAR

Mrs. Tice was right: marriage with Allen was out of the question. He could not make the daughter of a murderer his wife; no power, human or divine, would sanction such a union. Dora no longer wondered at Allen's strange silence. It was natural that he should shrink from telling her so terrible a story, and from branding her father with the terrible name of assassin. She remembered how she had been glad to know that her father had died without killing Edermont; that he had gone to his account without blood on his hands. No wonder Pallant had chuckled at her ignorance, and had forborne to enlighten her. George Carew had taken a life in cold blood, with deliberation and malice aforethought. She, Dora Carew, was the daughter of a criminal.

Dora said little to Mrs. Tice after the story had been told. Indeed, there was nothing to say; for she knew her fate only too well. She could never marry Allen; and if she did not become Joad's wife, to save her lover from arrest, and possibly condemnation, she would be forced to remain single for the rest of her life, lonely and sorrowful. The sins of the father had been visited on the child, and Dora was reaping the harvest of blood which George Carew had sown. Morally speaking, the end of all things had come to Dora.

"I shall go over to Canterbury with you," she said to Mrs. Tice, "and say good-bye to Allen. I can never marry him; but I can at least see him for the last time, and tell him that he is safe from Joad."

"But, my dear young lady, you will not marry that wicked man?"

"If I can save Allen in no other way, I must," said Dora firmly. "Consider his position, Mrs. Tice, should Joad accuse him of the crime! He quarrelled with Edermont, he came here at the very hour of the murder, and when he left the house Edermont was dead. To all this circumstantial evidence he can oppose only his bare word. I tell you he is in danger of being hanged, Mrs. Tice. Nothing is left for me to do save to marry Joad. He dare not speak then."

"The real assassin may be found yet," suggested Mrs. Tice hopefully.

"There is little chance of that, I am afraid. When all these hundreds of men, stimulated by that gigantic reward, have failed to track the murderer, how can I hope to succeed? No, Mrs. Tice; the name of the criminal will never be known, so it only remains for me to see Allen for the last time, and return here to be Joad's wife."

The housekeeper sighed. This indeed appeared the sole way out of the difficulty, and she could offer no advice on the subject. It went to her heart that Dora should marry so disreputable a creature; but as the reason for such marriage was the safety of Allen Scott, she was content that it should take place. In her love for Allen, the old nurse would have sacrificed a hundred women. Dora's fate was hard; she admitted that, but it was necessary.

Allen proved less ill than they expected to find him. He was annoyed that Mrs. Tice had been sent for, although he was glad to see both her and Dora. Nevertheless, he protested against being considered a sick man, or that he should take to his bed.

"I'm not well enough to go about my work," he said candidly; "at the same time, I am not sufficiently ill to retire to a sick-room. I shall be all right in a day or two."

He did not look as though he would recover in so short a time. In default of bed, he was lying on a sofa in the dining-room, covered with a rug, and he appeared to be thoroughly ill. His eyes were bright, his hands were burning, and every now and again he shivered with cold, as though suffering from an attack of ague. Mrs. Tice made him some beef-tea, and insisted upon his taking it, which he did after much persuasion.

"You see, Dora," he said, with a smile, "the doctor has to be prescribed for by his old nurse. All my science and knowledge goes for nothing in comparison with Mrs. Tice's remedies."

"I know what is common-sense," said Mrs. Tice, smiling also. "Lie still, Mr. Allen, and keep warm. Miss Carew will sit with you here while I look after the house. I dare say it has been dreadfully neglected in my absence."

"That is hardly a compliment to my management," said Allen, trying to smile.

"Oh, as to that, no gentleman can look after a house, Mr. Allen. It's woman's work to see to such things. Let me manage at present, and when I am gone your wife can take my place."

"Wife!" echoed Dr. Scott, with a sigh. "I shall never marry."

Dora said nothing, but bent her head to hide the despair written on her face. Feeling that she had said too much, Mrs. Tice hastened to excuse herself; in doing so, she only succeeded in making matters worse. The name of Joad occurred in the midst of her excuses, and Allen made a feeble gesture of displeasure.

"I wish you would not mention that creature," he said, clasping Dora's hand. "I hate him as much as Dora does. He is her enemy and mine."

"But, for all that, I must marry him, Allen."

"No. You must not sacrifice yourself."

"Mr. Allen, be sensible!" cried Mrs. Tice. "You stand in a dreadful position; you are at the mercy of Joad. Should he speak you are lost."

"I can tell my story."

Dora shook her head.

"It will not be believed in the face of Joad's evidence," said she dolefully. "And then the quarrel you had with Mr. Edermont gives colour to his accusation."

Dr. Scott made a gesture of dissent, but Mrs. Tice supported Dora.

"She is right, Mr. Allen. If Joad speaks you are lost. Talk it over with Miss Carew, sir, and I'll hear what you think when I come back. Just now I must look after the house."

When she left the room, Allen waited until the door was closed, then turned to look at Dora. She was sitting by the side of the sofa with a drooping head, and a sad expression on her face. Moved by her silent sorrow, and ascribing it rightly to the unhappy position in which they stood to one another, he took her hands within his own.

"Do not look so sad, Dora," he said softly; "I shall be better shortly. It is the knowledge of what was told to me by Mr. Edermont which has made me ill. But I shall recover, my dear, and bear my troubles like a man."

Dora burst into tears.

"I can only bear my troubles like a woman," she sobbed. "Oh, Allen, Allen! what have we done, you and I, that we should be made so unhappy? You are in a very dangerous position, and I can save you only by marrying a man I detest."

"Dora, you must not marry Joad. I cannot accept safety at the price of your lifelong misery."

"What does it matter about my marrying that creature?" she said, drying her tears. "I can never become your wife."

Allen groaned.

"True, true; ah, how true it is that the sins of the father are visited on the children! It is shameful that we should suffer as we do for the evil of others."

"We cannot help our position, Allen. There is no hope."

"You are right," said Allen in a despairing tone; "there is no hope. Ah, Dora, if you only knew the truth!"

"I do know the truth."

"Who told you?" he asked, sitting up with a look of astonishment.

"Lady Burville told me that——"

"Lady Burville!" he interrupted sharply; "what does she know?"

"Everything. And it is no wonder, seeing that she is the root of all the evil."

"How do you mean that she is the root of all the evil?"

"Lady Burville is my mother, Allen."

"Great heavens! Your mother—Mrs. Carew!"

"Yes. Mrs. Carew, Mrs. Dargill, Lady Burville—whatever you like to call her. I know her story, Allen, and what she failed to relate Mrs. Tice told. I know that my father killed yours, and that we can never marry."

"Lady Burville—your mother told you this!" he stammered; "and I was so careful to hide the truth from you!"

"I know you spared me, in the goodness of your heart, Allen, but it was better that I should know the truth. Yes, I went up to town; I restored the pearl brooch to Lady Burville—I cannot call her my mother—and I heard her story."

"Dora!" Allen seized her hand again. "Did your mother kill Mr. Edermont?"

"No. Thank God, she is innocent of that crime!"

"Then how was it I found her brooch by the dead body?"

"She dropped it in the room when she went to see Mr. Edermont on that night."

"But why did she see Edermont?"

"He sent for her to deliver up a packet of letters she had written to him. It is a long story, Allen, and a sad one. Listen, and I will tell you all."

Allen signified his desire to hear the story, and listened eagerly while she told him what her mother had related. To make the information complete, Dora passed on to the history of the murder, as told by Mrs. Tice. When she finished, and Allen was in possession of all the facts, she waited for him to comment thereon. This he was not long in doing.

"I see that you know all, Dora," he said with a melancholy smile. "Yes, this is what Mr. Edermont told me on that day. I lost my head when he ended; I believe I advanced towards him in a threatening manner, to thrash him for the share he had taken in the matter. It was then that he threw up the window and cried out that I wished to kill him. Probably I was wrong to act as I did, as the miserable little creature was not responsible for the death of my father; but I did not consider that at the moment. When he cried out to you and Joad, I left the room, and the house. You remember, I would not speak to you when I went. I could not, my dear; the revelation had proved too much for my self-control. I felt half-mad, for I saw that I had lost you for ever."

"And why did you go up to London?" asked Dora anxiously.

"Edermont referred me to a file of the Morning Planet, containing an account of the tragedy which ended in the death of my father."

"You went up to see an account of your father's murder?"

"Yes. I could not bring myself to believe that matters were so bad as he made out. But in London I went to the office of the paper; I turned up the report, and it was true enough. Your father shot mine, as was stated by Edermont. Afterwards I went down to Christchurch, and found out the rest of the story from an old housekeeper."

"Did you learn that Lady Burville was my mother?"

"No: nor did Edermont tell me so. Why, I do not know. He only stated the bare facts of the case, and how my father had been killed. Now you know why I told you nothing, Dora—why I kept silent. I was afraid lest your father should be arrested for the double murder, and bring shame and pain on you, my poor dear."

"The double murder?"

"Yes. George Carew killed my father; and, in accordance with his oath, I believe he murdered Mr. Edermont—found him out after many years and killed him."

"You are wrong, Allen. I told you how Pallant blackmailed my mother, and learnt the whole story from my wretched father. Well, Captain Carew died two years ago in San Francisco."

"Are you sure?"

"I am certain. He died in Mr. Pallant's arms. Pallant has no reason to lie over that story."

"Then, if Carew did not kill Edermont, who did?"

"Ah," said Dora with a weary sigh, "that is just what we must find out, if only to save your life and prevent my marrying Joad."

"Dora," said Allen after a pause, "do you know why Pallant wanted that packet of letters?"

"Yes. He desired to confirm his possession of my mother. By threatening to show the letters to Sir John Burville, he hoped to get whatever money he wished."

"The scoundrel! What particular information did the letters contain to render them so valuable?"

"I don't know. Mr. Pallant hinted that they were about me."

"About you?" Allen reflected for a few moments. "Dora," he said at length, "I dare say those letters passed between your mother and your guardian after the tragedy at Christchurch. Probably they contained a full account of the crime, and details as to how your mother parted with you. In fact, I believe they contained a summary of Lady Burville's life. If Pallant had obtained those letters, no wonder he could have extorted money. If they had been shown to Sir John Burville, his wife—your mother—could have denied nothing. Her own handwriting would prove the falsity of her denial."

"I quite understand," said Dora; "but Mr. Edermont was wise enough to give them to my mother himself."

"And that is just it!" cried Allen. "Supposing Lady Burville had unconsciously let Pallant know that she was going to the Red House to receive the letters; supposing he followed her, and was too late to intercept the packet. Do you think he might have killed Edermont in a fit of rage at losing the letters?"

"No, Allen, I do not think so for a moment. Mr. Pallant is too cautious to act so foolishly. Besides, if it was as you say, he could easily have followed Lady Burville along that lonely road, and have forced her to give him the letters. No. Whoever killed my guardian, it was not Mr. Pallant."

"Then who is guilty?" asked Allen in despair.

"Ah!" said Dora with a melancholy sigh. "That secret is worth fifty thousand pounds and your life, my dear Allen."

CHAPTER XXII

WHAT DORA DISCOVERED

When Dora took leave of Allen, she returned to the Red House with the firm conviction that to save the doctor she would be obliged to marry Joad. In the face of this old man's evidence, she did not see how Allen could defend himself. It was true that he could produce the letter of Mr. Edermont, giving him a midnight invitation to his study; but such production would not mend matters. It would only show that he had been present at the very hour of the murder, and would confirm the evidence of Joad. Once that was proved, what plea could he put forward to prove his innocence? None. A quarrel might have taken place on the subject of their previous conversation, and Allen might have killed Edermont in a fit of rage. That was the view, Dora truly believed, which the judge and jury would take of the matter. And on the face of it what view could be more reasonable?

It was no use bringing Lady Burville into the question, for her evidence could throw no light on the subject. When she left the house Edermont was alive; when Scott arrived the old man was dead, and there was nothing to show that anyone had been in the study between Lady Burville's departure and Dr. Scott's arrival. Medical evidence could prove that Lady Burville was too feeble a woman to strike so terrible a blow, of too nervous a character to carry out so brutal a crime. No; if Lady Burville came into court, it would be to save herself, and to condemn Allen. Under these circumstances, it only remained to hush the matter up by granting Joad's wish. Dora hated the man, but for the sake of Allen she decided to marry him. Yet, as she still had a few days' grace before giving him his answer, she resolved to say nothing of her resolution at present. It might be that in the interval the real criminal might be discovered.

All that night Dora tossed and tossed on her bed, courting sleep in vain. She was like a rat in a trap, running round and round in the endeavour to escape. She would have done anything rather than consent to this marriage with Joad; but unless some miracle intervened, she saw no chance of escaping the ceremony. To be saddled with such a husband! to live in constant companionship with such a satyr! The poor girl wept bitterly at the very thought.

What would she feel when Joad demanded payment of the price of his silence?

Towards morning she fell into an uneasy slumber, and awoke more despondent than ever. It was with a listless air that she descended to breakfast, and only with a strong effort could she force herself to eat. Meg Gance, who brought in the meal, informed her Mr. Joad was already in the library, engrossed in his daily occupation.

"He come here afore nine," said Meg, who was a large, stupid countrywoman, with more muscle than brains; "it wasn't so when master lived, was it, Miss Dora?"

"No. But I don't suppose it matters much now when Mr. Joad comes, Meg."

"I dunno 'bout that," said the servant, putting her large hands on her hips; "it takes long to clean up bookshop, it do. I rarely get it done afore nine. I declare, miss, when Mr. Joad come this morn, I couldn't believe 'twas so late. Thought I, Clock's gone wrong again."

"What clock?" asked Dora, remembering the strange remark made by Pallant.

"Lor, miss, how sharp you speak!" said Meg, rather startled by the abruptness of the question. "Why, clock in hall, for sure!"

"Was it ever wrong, Meg?"

"A whole hour, miss; though how it could have lost hour in night I dunno. But it was ten when I looked at it in morning, while kitchen clock was nine. Too fast by hour, Miss Dora."

"On what night was it wrong?" asked Dora, eagerly feeling that she was on the verge of a discovery.

"Why, miss, it went wrong on night master had head bashed. Not as I wonder, miss, for my aunt had husband as died, and clock—her clock, miss—struck thirteen. Seems as clock knows of deaths and funerals," concluded Meg reflectively.

"Was the clock in the hall wrong by an hour when you saw it in the morning after the crime had been committed?"

"For sure, Miss Dora. But Lor' bless you, miss, it don't matter. I jes' put it right by kitchen clock, as has never lost a minute since I came here, and that's six years, miss."

"Why did you not mention that the clock was wrong when you gave your evidence?"

Meg stared at her mistress.

"I never thought, miss," she said gravely; "and I wasn't asked about clock. It didn't matter, I hope?"

"No," replied Dora carelessly, "it didn't matter. You need say nothing about it to Mr. Joad, or, indeed, to anyone."

"I aren't much of a chat at any time, miss," cried Meg, tossing her head; "and as for Mr. Joad, I'd as lief speak to blackbeetle! I won't say naught, bless you, no, miss."

"Very well, Meg. You can clear away."

This Meg did with considerable clatter and clamour; while Dora left the room, and without putting on a hat walked slowly across the lawn, in the dewy freshness of the morning. On reaching the beehive chair under the cedar, which was Joad's favourite outdoor study, the girl sat down, and looked contemplatively at the scene before her. A space of sunlit lawn, with a girdle of flaming rhododendrons fringing it on the right; tall poplars, musical with birds, bordering the ivy-draped wall; and beyond the wall itself the red-tiled roof of Joad's cottage, showing in picturesque contrast against the delicate azure of an August sky. After regarding the scene to right and left, as it lay steeped in the yellow sunlight, Dora's gaze finally rested on the glimpse of Joad's house. There it stayed; and her thoughts reverted to the remark about the clock made by Pallant, and to the later explanation given by Meg Gance. What connection these things had with Joad may be gathered from the girl's thoughts.

They ran something after this fashion: "Could it be possible that Joad had killed Edermont? There seemed to be no motive for his committing the crime, and he was not the kind of man to run needlessly into danger. Yet the discovery about the clock was certainly very strange. I knew it was correct on the night of the murder," meditated Dora. "I set my watch by it before I went upstairs. That was at half-past nine, and my watch has been right ever since. When Meg looked at it in the morning, it was an hour wrong; therefore, somebody must have put it wrong with intent. It is impossible that so excellent a clock could suddenly slip for an hour, and then go on again. Could Joad have been in the house on that night, and have put it on an hour? At the time of the murder the clock struck one, and at that hour Joad, according to his own showing and Mr. Pride's corroboration, was in the cottage. If the clock had been put wrong, the murder must have taken place at twelve, since it was an hour fast in the morning. There was ample time for Joad to commit the crime at twelve, and be back in his cottage by one."

Dora got up, and walked restlessly to and fro. She could not quite understand why the clock should have been put on an hour, so as to give a false time, when there was no one to hear it in the night. That she had woke up and heard it strike was quite an accident, although there had been nights when she had heard every hour, every chime, strike till dawn. Suddenly she remembered that once she had said something to Joad about her sleepless nights. On the impulse of the moment she walked into the library.

"Mr. Joad," she said to the old man, who was reading near the window, "that hall clock."

It seemed to Dora that a pallor crept over the red face of the man she addressed. However, he looked up quietly enough, and spoke to her with the greatest calmness.

"What about the hall clock, Miss Dora?" he asked in a puzzled tone.

"It is disturbing me again. I really must have it removed. In the dead hours I hear it strike in the most ghostly, graveyard fashion. As it did on that night," she concluded under her breath.

"Do you have many sleepless nights now?"

"How do you know that I have sleepless nights at all?" she asked quickly.

Joad looked at her in surprise.

"You told me so yourself shortly before we lost Julian," he said quietly. "It was toothache, was it not?"

"Yes—something of that sort," she answered carelessly. "But it is not toothache now. Still, I lie awake thinking."

"Of me?" said Joad with a leer.

"The week is not yet over, Mr. Joad," she said coldly; "till the end of it you have no right to ask me such a question. Good-bye for the present; I am going out on my bicycle."

This was an excuse. Confident that Joad had altered the clock, on the chance that she would hear it during her sleepless nights, she was confident also that for such reason, and for a more terrible one, he had been in the house on the night of the murder.

"He put on the clock so as to prove an alibi," she thought, wheeling her bicycle down the path to the gate. "If he killed Edermont at twelve o'clock—the right time when it struck one—he would have ample opportunity of getting back to his cottage through the postern. I quite believe that he was with Pride at one o'clock; but I also believe he was in the study at twelve."

She had proved to her own satisfaction that Joad could have been in the house; she wished to discover if he had killed Edermont. The assassin had committed the crime to obtain the manuscript containing the story of her guardian's life. If Joad were guilty, that manuscript would be in his possession. This was why Dora excused herself on a plea of riding her bicycle. She was determined to search Joad's cottage, and find out if the manuscript was hidden there.

With this intent she hid the bicycle behind the hedge on the other side of the road, and went to the cottage. There was plenty of time for her to search, as Joad took his mid-day meal in the Red House and never returned to his house until nine at night. She had the whole day at her disposal, and determined to search in every corner for the manuscript she believed he had hidden. If she found it, she would then be able to prove Allen guiltless and Joad guilty. It would be a magnificent revenge on her part. The man would be caught in his own trap.

It can be easily guessed by what steps Dora had arrived at this conclusion—the chance remark of Pallant anent the possibility of the clock being wrong; the chance explanation of Meg which proved that the clock was an hour fast on the morning after the murder had taken place; the memory of her own remark to Joad about her sleepless nights; and the conclusion that the old man had put the clock wrong for purposes of his own. The inference to be drawn from these facts was that Joad had been in the house on the night of the second of August. If he had been in the house, it was probable that he had killed Edermont, since Allen and Lady Burville, the only other people who had been present at the same hour, were innocent. It had been proved by sundry scraps of evidence that the murder had been committed to obtain possession of the manuscript. Therefore, if Joad were guilty, he must have hidden the fruits of his crime. Where? In the cottage, without doubt.

The front door of the cottage was locked, so Dora went round to the back. She knew that Joad was in the habit of hiding the key of the back door under the water-butt, and sure enough she found it there. To open the door and pass into his study was the work of a moment. So here she was in the stronghold of the enemy. But where was the manuscript?

The room was not very large, and lined on all four sides with books. A writing-desk, littered with papers, stood before the single window, and a few chairs were scattered round. There were also a horsehair sofa, a small sideboard of varnished deal, three or four china ornaments, and a little clock on the mantelpiece. The floor was covered with straw matting, but what the pattern of the paper was like no one could tell, for it was hidden completely by the books. The whole apartment looked penurious in the extreme and very untidy. Books lay on chairs and sofas, and the fireplace was filled with torn-up letters, newspapers, and hastily scribbled manuscripts.

"The books first," decided Dora, after a look at this chaos.

There was no need to go through them one by one, for dust lay thickly upon bindings and shelves. She had only to glance to see those which had been disturbed within the last few weeks. Those that had been taken down she examined carefully, but could find no trace of the manuscript. She looked on the top of the bookcase, went down on her knees to search the lower shelves, and still found nothing. At the end of an hour Dora had gone through the whole library of Joad, but had come across no trace of the wished-for paper. He had hidden it—always presuming that it was in his possession—more cunningly than she had thought.

"Now for the desk."

Another hour's search in drawers and pigeonholes and blotting-pad likewise revealed nothing. Dora emptied out the wastepaper basket, and sorted every scrap, and still she was unsuccessful. Then she lifted portions of the matting, removed the cushions of the chairs, searched the sideboard, and dived into the recesses of the sofa. All to no purpose.

"Perhaps he has not got it after all," thought Dora, disappointed, "or he has burnt it."

Burning suggested the fireplace; but she saw that there had not been a fire for months in the grate. It then struck her that Mr. Joad might have taken an idea from Poe's "Purloined Letter," and have hidden the manuscript in some conspicuous place. The fireplace alone was unsearched, so she went down on her knees and turned out the disorderly mass of papers. Her patience was rewarded at last. From under the heap she drew forth a crumpled mass of paper, foolscap size, and spread it out carefully. Then she uttered a cry. "The Confession of Julian Dargill, better known as Julian Edermont," she read. "Ah! I was right. Here is the stolen story of the past, and Joad is the man who killed my guardian."

CHAPTER XXIII

THE MADNESS OF LAMBERT JOAD

With the recovered manuscript in her hands, with the knowledge where it had been found, and with the memory of the clock being wrong, Dora felt convinced that Joad was guilty of the crime. Without doubt he had designed to kill Edermont on that night, and had prepared the alibi so as to prove his innocence should such proof be needed. But what was his motive for the perpetration of so detestable a crime? Why had he stolen the manuscript, and why had he not destroyed so dangerous a piece of evidence? Dora believed that the answer to these questions was to be found in the manuscript itself. The reading of it would probably solve the whole mystery.

Having accomplished her task, she slipped the paper into the pocket of her dress, ran out of the house, and, having locked the door, repaired to the place where she had hidden her bicycle. To give colour to her excuse to Joad, she mounted and rode down the road for some considerable distance. Indeed, she felt inclined there and then to go to Canterbury and assure Allen that he was safe, and that she had won a fortune by discovering the actual criminal; but her desire to do away with any possible suspicions on the part of Joad induced her to abandon such intention. When he found the manuscript gone, he might suspect her if she went directly into Canterbury, whereas, if she behaved as usual, he could have no doubts on the subject.

"Besides," said Dora to herself, as she turned her face towards Chillum, "Joad never goes to his cottage during the day, and therefore he will not find out his loss until to-night. Should he suspect that I have discovered his secret, he may do me an injury, or take to flight. I must allay his suspicions, and see Allen about the manuscript. We will read it together, and then take such steps as may be necessary to save him and arrest Joad."

On approaching the gates of the Red House, Dora received a shock, for on glancing at Joad's cottage, she saw its owner coming out of the door. Perhaps her questions about the clock had induced him to depart from his usual routine, and by rousing his suspicions had created a desire to assure himself that the manuscript was safe; but whatever might be the reason, Dora had never known Joad to revisit his domicile in the daytime. A qualm seized her lest he should guess what she had done; but the memory of what was at stake nerved her to resistance, and she confronted the approaching old man with a mien cool and composed. Certainly she needed all her courage at that moment, for Joad was conducting himself like a lunatic.

His face was redder than usual with suppressed rage; he swung round his arms in a threatening manner, and, hardly seeing her in his blind fury, babbled about his loss. Dora did not need to hear his words to be assured that he had discovered the loss of the manuscript. But she strained her ears to listen, in the hope that Joad might say something likely to incriminate himself.

"Lost, lost!" muttered Joad, as he shuffled near her—"and after all my care. What am I to do now? What—what—what?"

"Is anything wrong, Mr. Joad?"

The man paused before Dora with a dazed look, and suddenly cooled down in the most surprising manner. Knowing the dangerous position in which he was placed by the loss of the manuscript, he saw the necessity for dissimulation. His rage gave place to smiles, his furious gestures to fawning.

"No, Miss Dora; there is nothing wrong. I have lost a precious book, that is all. But I know who took it," he broke out with renewed fury.

Dora felt nervous, and for the moment she thought that he suspected her. But the next moment—still talking of the manuscript under the flimsy disguise of a book—his words reassured her. "Oh yes," he repeated; "I know who stole it, but I'll be revenged;" then he shook his fists in the air, as though invoking a curse on someone, and returned to the Red House.

When Dora reached her own room, she took out the manuscript. It was a lengthy effusion, evidently carefully prepared, and certainly clearly written. With a thrill of excitement the girl sat down to read the story, and learn from it, if possible, the motive of Joad in becoming a midnight assassin. Before she had read two lines, Meg knocked at her door. Dora hid away the precious paper hastily in her wardrobe, and called on Meg to enter.

"Dinner is up, miss," said the stout countrywoman, "and Mr. Joad waits. He don't look well, Miss Dora. Sheets ain't nothing to face of he."

"Is he in a bad temper, Meg?"

"Lordy, no, miss! He ghastly pale and quiet like."

Meg's report proved to be true. Joad's rage had died out into a subdued nervousness, and his red face had paled to a yellowish hue. He said little and ate little, but Dora noticed that he drank more than his ordinary allowance of whisky-and-water. Every now and then he cast a furtive glance round the room, as though waiting anxiously for the unexpected to happen. His conduct reminded Dora of the late Mr. Edermont's behaviour in church during the Litany, and there was no doubt in her mind as to Joad's feelings. He had received a shock, and in consequence thereof he was thoroughly frightened.

Towards the end of the meal he grew more composed, under the influence of the spirits and water, and it was then that he abruptly informed Dora that he was going into Canterbury.

"You are going into Canterbury," she echoed, fairly astonished, "this afternoon?"

"Yes; I have not been in the town for months. But I wish to consult—a lawyer."

"About the loss of your book, I suppose?"

Joad raised his heavy eyes, and sent a piercing glance in her direction.

"Yes," he said, in a quiet tone, "I wish to consult about that loss."

"Will you see Mr. Carver?"

"On the whole," said Joad, with great deliberation, "I think I shall see Mr. Carver. He knows much; he may as well know more."

"What do you mean?" asked Dora, startled by the significance of this speech.

"You will know to-morrow, Miss Carew."

He left the room, and shortly afterwards the house. Anxious to learn if he intended to fly, and so escape the consequences of his crime, Dora followed him down to the gate. This had not been kept locked of late, and Joad swung it easily open. Stepping out, he cast a glance to right and left in an uneasy fashion, and suddenly staggered against the wall with his hand to his heart. In an instant Dora was beside him.

"What is the matter, Mr. Joad?"

"Only the old trouble—my heart, my heart," he muttered; "it will kill me some day. The sooner the better—now."

Dora took this speech as an acknowledgment of his guilt, and withdrew a little from his neighbourhood. Joad took no notice of this shrinking, but explained his plans.

"I go to my cottage to change my clothes," he said calmly, "then I will get a trap from the hotel, and drive to Canterbury to see Mr. Carver. You need not expect me at the Red House to-night, Miss Dora. I shall stay in my own cottage. It will not do for me to be out after dark."

"Why not, Mr. Joad? You are in no danger?"

"I am in danger of losing my life," retorted the old man, and, flinging her detaining hand rudely aside, he ran across the road with an activity surprising in one of his years and sedentary life.

When he disappeared Dora returned to the house. She was at a loss what to do with regard to Joad. His actions and speech were so strange that she was afraid lest he should fly. If he did, his complicity in the crime might never be proved, and so Allen's safety might be compromised. Dora was determined that this should not be. She decided to get into Canterbury before Joad, to see Mr. Carver and ask his advice; afterwards to call on Allen and show him the manuscript. In some way or other she would contrive to circumvent the discovered villain.

Having come to this decision, Dora put the manuscript in her pocket, assumed her hat and gloves, and took out her bicycle. Joad was not yet out of his cottage, so she hurried in hot haste, and spun up the road at full speed. By the time he had got to the hotel and ordered the trap she hoped to be in Canterbury preparing the ground for his arrival, so that his efforts to fly—if indeed he intended to do so—might be baffled in every direction. Dora felt that a crucial moment was at hand, and that it behoved her to have all her wits about her if she hoped to save Allen and win the fifty thousand pounds.

On her arrival at Canterbury, Dora lost no time in seeking the lawyer. He was busy in his dingy back office as usual, and betrayed no surprise at seeing his visitor. With a dry smile he shook hands, and placed a chair for her, then he gave his explanation of her appearance.

"You have come to ask further about your five hundred pounds," said he; "if so, I am afraid you are wasting your time."

"I do not intend to waste my time on that matter, Mr. Carver," replied Dora quietly, "nor yours either. The object of my visit is far more important. I have discovered who killed Mr. Edermont."

If she hoped to astonish Mr. Carver by this speech, she was never more mistaken in her life. He did not display any surprise, but merely laughed and rubbed his dry hands together.

"Have I, then, to congratulate you on gaining fifty thousand pounds?" he asked satirically.

"You can judge for yourself, Mr. Carver," said Dora quietly; and then and there, without further preamble, she related the finding of the manuscript, the behaviour of Joad, and the evidence of the clock.

Carver betrayed his interest by frequent raisings of his eyebrows, but otherwise remained motionless until the conclusion of her story. She might as well have been speaking to a stone.

"And this manuscript," he asked; "have you it with you?"

"Yes," Dora laid it on the table, "here it is. The story of Mr. Edermont's early life."

"You have read it?"

"No; not yet. I have not had time to do so. I have brought it in to read with Allen—that is, unless you require it."

Carver thought for a moment, and shook his head.

"No," he said in an amiable tone, "I do not require it at the present moment. I shall see Mr. Joad first, and then call on Dr. Scott to hear his and your report on this paper."

"Do you think Mr. Joad is guilty?" asked Dora, replacing the manuscript in her pocket.

"Circumstantial evidence is strongly against him," replied Mr. Carver cautiously, "but I shall reserve my opinion until I hear his story."

"Do you think he will call on you?"

"He told you that he intended to do so, Miss Carew."

"Very true, Mr. Carver. All the same, he may have done so to save time. For all we know, he may design to go straight to the railway-station and catch the London express."

"Oh, I can frustrate that scheme," said Carver, rising. "Mr. Joad's conduct is sufficiently suspicious to justify his detention on the ground of complicity, if not of actual guilt. A word to Inspector Jedd, and Mr. Joad will not get away by the express. Go and see Dr. Scott, my dear young lady, and leave me to deal with your friend."

"You won't let him escape?"

"No," said Carver dryly. "On the whole, I had rather you got the fifty thousand pounds than anyone else."

And then he conducted Dora to the door with a courtesy he had never extended before to any female client, and at which his clerks were greatly astonished. Congratulating herself on having thus made all safe, Dora went to see Allen. He was still unwell, but felt better than he had done on the previous day. He was surprised at her visit, and gathered from her bright looks that she had something of importance to communicate to him.

"What is it, Dora?" he asked anxiously; "good or bad news?"

"Good! You are safe!"

"Then you intend to marry Joad?" said Allen in a tone of despair.

"Indeed, I intend no such thing! Mr. Joad has other things to think about besides marriage."

"What other things?"

"How to save his neck. Yes, you may well look astonished, Allen. Joad, and none other, killed my guardian! Here is the proof!" and Dora flung the manuscript on the table.

CHAPTER XXIV

THE STOLEN MANUSCRIPT

Allen looked on the manuscript thus suddenly produced in mute wonder. With a swift glance he questioned Dora as to what it was—for he could not yet bring himself to believe that it was the lost paper—and how she had come by it. The girl afforded him at once a concise explanation.

"It is the paper containing an account of the early life of Mr. Edermont," said she, with a nod; "the manuscript stolen from the bureau, on account of which we believe the murder to have been perpetrated. I found it in the cottage of Joad."

"In the cottage of Joad?" echoed Allen slowly. "How did he come by it?"

"By robbery and murder. He is the guilty person."

"Dora—are you sure? He proved an alibi, you know."

"I am aware of that, and I am aware also how he prepared such alibi. It is a long story, Allen. I shall tell it to you, and then we will read the manuscript together."

"I am all attention," cried Allen, settling himself on the sofa. "Go on, you most wonderful girl."

"I am a most unfortunate girl," said Dora sadly. "By my discovery I have saved you from arrest, and perhaps condemnation, and myself from a marriage which revolted me. But what is left after all, my dear? Nothing, nothing. We can never be anything but friends to one another, for our lives have been ruined by the sins of other people. It is cruelly hard."

"You speak only too truly, Dora," said Allen, taking her hand. "And I can give you no comfort; I can give myself no consolation. Your father's crime has parted us, and we must suffer vicariously for his guilt."

For a moment or so they remained silent, thinking over the hopelessness of their position. But matters were too important and pressing to admit of much time being wasted in useless lamentations. Dora was the first to recover her speech, and forthwith related the events of the day, from the conversation of Meg Gance down to the visit to Carver. Allen interrupted her frequently with exclamations of surprise.

"You are right, Dora!" he cried when she had ended. "How wonderfully you have worked out the matter! Without doubt Joad was hidden in the house while Lady Burville saw Edermont. After she left, he must have killed his friend, and secured the manuscript. No doubt he hid again when he heard me coming, and saw me, not in the road, as he alleges, but in the study. Oh, the villain! and he would have saved his neck at the expense of mine!"

"He had not even that excuse, Allen; for, owing to his manipulation of the hall clock, there was absolutely no suspicion that he was guilty. He accused you to gain me, but now I have caught him in his own trap, and no doubt Mr. Carver will have him arrested this night."

"I hope so," said Dr. Scott angrily; "he is a wicked old ruffian! But I cannot understand why he killed Mr. Edermont."

"The manuscript may inform us," said Dora, taking it up. "Let us read it at once."

Allen consented eagerly, and Dora, smoothing the pages, began to read what may be termed the confession of Julian Dargill, alias Edermont. Some parts of the narrative were concisely told, others expanded beyond all due bounds; and as a literary attempt the story was a failure. But for style or elegance of language the young couple cared little. They wished to learn the truth, and they found it in the handwriting of the dead man.

"'My name is Julian Dargill,'" began the manuscript abruptly. "'I was born at Christchurch, in Hants, where my family lived for many generations. My parents died whilst I was at Oxford, and at the age of twenty I found myself my own master. For ten years I travelled in the company of a young man whom I had met at the University. He was not a gentleman, but he had a clever brain, and was an amusing companion, so I paid his expenses for the pleasure of his conversation and company. When I returned home, I left Mallison—for such was his name, John Mallison—in my London rooms, and came down to my house at Christchurch. Here I took up my residence, and here I fell in love with Laura Burville. She was a charming blonde, delicate and tiny as a fairy, full of life and vivacity. Her face was singularly beautiful, her figure perfection, and she had the gift of bringing sunshine wherever she went. Needless to say, I fell deeply in love with her, and would have made her my wife but for the foolish behaviour of her parents. These were religious fanatics of peculiarly rigid principles, and they disapproved of my tendency to a gay life. How they came to have so charming a daughter I could never understand. Miss Treherne—or shall I call her by the fonder name of Laura?—had three suitors—myself, Dr. Scott, a widower, and Captain George Carew, of the merchant service. Scott was a handsome and clever man, but poor, and reckless in his way of life. His wife had died when his son Allen was born, and Scott left the child to be brought up by the nurse while he went flirting with all the pretty girls in the country. Mr. and Mrs. Treherne disapproved of him also on account of this behaviour. So far as I saw, neither Dr. Scott nor myself had any chance of marrying Laura, for her parents favoured the suit of her third admirer, George Carew. I hated and feared that man. He was a brutal sailor, with a vindictive spirit and an unusually violent temper. Everybody yielded to his imperious spirit, and he rode rough-shod over any opposition that might be made to his wishes. He fell in love with Laura, and determined to marry her. At my pretensions and those of Scott he laughed scornfully, and warned both that he would permit neither of us to interfere with his design. He was cunning enough to ingratiate himself with the parents of Laura by pretending to be religious, and ostensibly became more of a fanatic than the Trehernes themselves. Laura was carried away by the violence of his wooing; her parents were delighted with his pretended conversion; and against their support and Laura's timidity—I can call her yielding by no other name—Scott and myself could do nothing. Carew married her. I omitted to state that Carew was not rich. He was part owner in a ship called the Silver Arrow, which traded to the Cape of Good Hope, and sometimes went as far as Zanzibar. When the marriage took place Carew was forced to take command of his ship for a voyage to the Cape. He wished Laura to go also, but this she refused to do, and by offering a dogged resistance to his violent temper she managed to get her own way for once. This I learnt from her afterwards. Alas! had she only been as determined over refusing marriage with Carew, all this sorrow might not have come upon us. But she was quite infatuated with the insolent sailor, and while he was with her I believe she loved him after a fashion. Nevertheless, I do not think her passion either for Carew or for myself was very strong. Leaving then for his voyage, Carew established his wife in a cottage near my house, and went away almost immediately after the honeymoon. Her parents had left Christchurch shortly before to take possession of some property in Antrim, Ireland, which had been left to them. Laura was quite alone, and found her state of grass-widowhood sufficiently tiresome. She wished for distraction, and encouraged myself and Dr. Scott to call upon her. As we were still in love with her, we accepted her invitation only too gladly, and for six months we devoted ourselves to her amusement. Then came the news that the Silver Arrow had been wrecked on the coast of Guinea. The information was brought by the first mate, who had been picked up in an open boat by a passing ship. His companions were dead of hardship and suffering, and it was only with the greatest difficulty that he was brought round again.

"'On his return to England he told his tale to the owners of the ship, and then communicated the news to Mrs. Carew. Without doubt her husband was drowned, and so after six months of married life she found herself a widow, but ill-provided with money. As part owner of the Silver Arrow, the dead Carew had some claim to a portion of the insurance; but, owing to some commercial and legal trickery, no money was obtainable from this source. Laura had barely sufficient to live on. It may be guessed what effect poverty had upon her refined and pleasure-loving nature. She refused to go to her parents in Ireland, as their gloomy religious views were alien to her more æsthetic leanings; yet she could not remain in Christchurch with hardly sufficient to sustain life. Dr. Scott offered to marry her, but he was too poor to give her the luxuries of life, and she refused to become his wife or step-mother to his little boy. Then I offered myself, and was accepted. I was not so handsome as Scott, or so manly and daring as her first husband; but I was rich, and while pretending to love me but little, she married me for my fortune. I was content to take her even on such terms, and we arranged to become husband and wife. Owing to the recent death of Carew, we could not marry openly in Christchurch; and as Laura had never truly loved the sailor, she did not care to pay a tribute to his hated memory by a year of mourning. Rather was she anxious to marry me at once, and for this purpose she went up to London. After a decent interval, to avert suspicion, I followed, and we were married shortly afterwards by special license in the church of St. Pancras. John Mallison was the best man, and arranged all the details for me. These things happened some months after Carew's supposed death. Then we travelled for a year, and at the end of it came back with our child Dora to Christchurch, where——"

"Our child?" said Dora, interrupting her reading. "What does that mean, Allen?"

"No doubt that Dargill adopted you as his child after the death of Carew."

"But I was his ward here; why does he not call me his ward in this manuscript?"

"Read on," said Allen. "You may discover the reason."

"'We took up our abode at my mansion in Christchurch,'" read Dora swiftly, "'and for a time we were fairly happy. But I was not altogether pleased with my wife. She did not love me, nor did she make any pretence to do so. Indeed, I believe she despised me for my weakness of body and amiability of temper. Dr. Scott began to call again, and Laura encouraged his visits. I forbade him the house, but my wife and himself defied me, and I was powerless to control their behaviour. One evening, after a scene with Laura, I left the house. Scott was in the habit of crossing the lawn at dusk and entering the drawing-room, to flirt with my wife while I was reading in the library. I also came the same way at times in preference to going round by the door; and one evening, entering thus, I chanced upon them. The discovery resulted in a violent scene; and next morning I left for London, vowing never to return until my wife dismissed Scott from her thoughts. The departure saved my life.

"'While I was away, Carew returned to Christchurch. He had been saved by some negroes on the Guinea Coast, and had been detained in captivity by them for over a year. Finally he escaped, managed to get to England, and came to claim his wife. When he heard of our marriage he went mad with rage. He accused me of corrupting his wife, of spreading a false report of his death, and finally swore that he would not rest until he had killed me. I verily believe that he was bent on doing so, notwithstanding my innocence in the matter; and had I not been absent in London, he would have shot me without mercy. As it was, he committed a murder in the hope of killing me.

"'My wife—as I must still call her—had no opportunity of warning me, as Carew kept such a close watch on her. He expected me to return, and took up his quarters in the house with the avowed intention of killing me. Laura sent for Scott to see how she could save me—rather for her own sake than for mine—and he came to see her one evening by stealth. Carew had heard from one of the servants that I was in the habit of crossing the lawn and entering the drawing-room. When he saw Scott approaching in the same direction he thought it was me; and, being provided with a pistol, which he always carried, he shot the man through the heart. When he found out whom he had killed, he fled, to escape being arrested; but his last words to Laura were that he would hunt me down and kill me.

"'All this came out at the inquest, which was reported in the Morning Planet under the heading of "A Romantic Tragedy." On hearing how my life was sought by Carew—still at large—I left my lodgings and went into hiding. What else could I do? I am a weak and puny man, and, morally speaking, I am a coward. It is not my fault. I was born so. I dared not face this brute in his ungoverned rage, and so I hid. Then John Mallison came to my rescue. He was rather like me, and he proposed to adopt my name and go to America, letting Carew know in some way how he had fled. Mallison was a brave man, and I knew that he could hold his own better than

I against Carew. He assumed my name, and I supplied him with funds. Carew saw him by chance in Regent Street, and in the distance took him for me. Mallison, to encourage this false recognition, fled to America, and Carew followed. Then I prepared for my own safety.

"'I took the name of Julian Edermont, and transferred my property in the funds to that name. I bought, through Carver, the Red House, near Canterbury, and I made it secure against robbers and my enemy Carew. Then I went to live there. I was afraid to go back to Laura—for whom I provided amply—lest Carew should hear of it. And I wrote to her about our child. Laura was not a good mother, and I was afraid she would neglect Dora. Some letters passed between us—while I was in London, for I did not give her my new address or name—and she ultimately sent Dora to me. Since then Dora has lived with me as my ward, for I was afraid to say that she was my daughter, lest Carew should find out.'"

"His adopted daughter, of course," interrupted Allen. "He was afraid your father might kill him, and take you away."

"'Later on I found my old college companion, Joad, starving in London, and took him to live with me,'" Dora went on. "'Mallison came back from America, and I provided for him likewise. So far I felt safe; but all these years I have had a belief that Carew would find me out, in spite of all my precautions, and kill me. If I am found murdered, George Carew will be the culprit, as no one else has any reason to wish for my death. I am at peace with all men. To punish him I leave by will the bulk of my fortune to him or her who finds out and punishes George Carew for his villainy. I hope my daughter Dora may be so fortunate. She need have no compunction in doing so, for Carew is not her father. She is my child, born of my marriage with Laura, and I only called her Carew, and my ward, to do away with any possible discovery by Carew. The certificate of her birth is with my family lawyer in Lincoln's Inn Fields.'"

"Dora!" cried Allen, starting up, "you are not Carew's daughter—not the daughter of the man who killed my father!"

"Edermont—Dargill—my father!" stammered Dora. "What does it mean?"

"Mean!" cried Allen, taking her in his arms—"that your father did not kill mine—and we can marry!"

CHAPTER XXV

CONFESSION

There was also a short note to the manuscript, stating that Edermont had found out and helped the son of his old enemy, Dr. Scott, on the ground that he felt himself to be the cause indirectly of the man's death. Allen took occasion to explain this particular matter.

"Now I come to look back on it," he said reflectively, "I believe that Edermont must have supplied most of the funds for my education. I understood they came from moneys left by my dead father; but from this story"—touching the manuscript—"it would appear that he died poor. Certainly Mr. Edermont behaved generously in inviting me to settle in Canterbury when I qualified for a doctor, and in helping me with a loan. I am afraid I acted badly to him on that day," added Allen, in a penitent tone, "but I was not myself; the news of my father's terrible death maddened me."

"And he was my father, after all!" sighed Dora. "Poor soul! I never cared over-much for him, as I did not like his personality. And, as I thought I was living on my own money, I did not realize his generosity. I am glad to know that I am not the daughter of Carew."

"It is strange that Mrs. Tice did not know Edermont was your father," said Allen, after a pause, "for you must have been born shortly before the Dargills returned to Christchurch. Ah, here is Mrs. Tice," he added, as the housekeeper entered. "Come here, nurse; we have good news for you."

"And what may that be?" asked the old dame, smiling.

"Dora and I intend to fulfil our engagement, and marry."

The face of Mrs. Tice grew stern with dismay and disapproval.

"Impossible, Mr. Allen! How can you marry the daughter of your father's murderer?"

"That is just it, nurse; Dora is not the daughter of Carew, but of Julian Dargill."

"Oh, she was adopted by Mr. Dargill, I know," said Mrs. Tice, still unconvinced, "and was called by his name in Christchurch. Why he changed her name to Carew I do not know, though, to be sure, she was his ward, and not his daughter, and Carew was her real name."

"So we all thought," said Dora impetuously; "but we have just discovered that I am really and truly the daughter of Mr. Dargill and his wife Laura. Listen, Mrs. Tice, and I'll tell you the story."

The narrative greatly surprised Mrs. Tice, who was forced to sit down and lift up her hands in her surprise. She was forced to believe that Dora was Dargill's daughter by Laura Carew's second marriage, and—as Mrs. Tice mentally noted—illegitimate, owing to Carew still being alive after her birth. But the housekeeper was too wise and kind-hearted to touch upon so delicate a point.

"Deary, deary me!" she ejaculated. "And no one knew it in Christchurch! I never saw you myself, Miss Dora, or I should have known that so young a child could not have been the daughter of a man dead over a year. I am surprised no one else guessed it. How blind we all are!"

"Oh, you may be sure Lady Burville told some story to account for the appearance and size of the child," said Allen cynically. "She is an adept at trickery. But I cannot understand, Dora, why she did not tell you the name of your real father."

"She did not wish to inculpate herself more than was necessary," said Dora, in a bitter tone. "She told me she was my mother only because she believed I would denounce her as guilty of the crime. And you know those letters Pallant wanted, Allen? Well, I have no doubt that those were the letters she wrote to Edermont—I can hardly bring myself to call him father—giving him permission to take me to live with him. Probably he paid her for doing so."

"After all, she is your mother, Miss Dora," said Mrs. Tice reprovingly.

"She has not acted a mother's part," retorted Dora. "She deserted me, she deceived me, she lied to me; I never wish to set eyes on her again."

"I think that will be rather a relief to her than otherwise," said Allen. "She is determined to keep her position as Sir John's wife, and will refuse to make any explanation likely to endanger it. However, it does not matter to us, my dear. The bar to our marriage is removed; indeed, I wonder your father did not tell me the truth."

"The poor soul was a coward, Allen. He admits as much in his confession. Few men would have behaved as he did, especially in the face of the fact that Captain Carew was in danger of arrest for the murder of your father. All Mr. Edermont's elaborate precautions were dictated solely by his lifelong dread. I can see no other reason why he should have passed me off as his ward. However, now that we know the truth, I can marry you."

"We will marry as soon as you like, dearest. And I am glad for your sake, Dora, that you will inherit the fifty thousand pounds left by your father."

"But how is that, Mr. Allen?" cried Mrs. Tice in amazement. "That money was only left to the person who discovered the murderer."

"Well, nurse, Dora has done so. Joad is the culprit."

"You don't say so! Well, I always did think he was a bad man. And he had the boldness to say you were guilty of his own wickedness!" cried Mrs. Tice indignantly. "I am glad he has fallen into his own trap. But why did he kill Mr. Dargill?"

"Ah," said Allen, "that is just what I should like to know. No motive is assigned in the manuscript. It is a mystery at present."

"Mr. Carver may force him to confess his reason," suggested Dora, "or perhaps he may guess it."

"What! Mr. Carver?"

"Yes, Mrs. Tice. I believe Mr. Carver knows a great deal more about my unhappy father than he chooses to confess. From the reference in the manuscript to my father's family lawyers, I am inclined to think that Mr. Carver knows who they are. If he does, he knows also that Mr. Edermont's real name was Julian Dargill."

"I wonder if he knows anything about John Mallison," said Allen abruptly.

"I don't see what there is to know about him," replied Dora carelessly; "the man did his work well, and inveigled Carew to America. When he returned my father recompensed him, as he says in his confession. I dare say John Mallison is settled somewhere in England, happy and content. Why do you ask, Allen?"

"I was thinking that failing Joad's confession Mallison might know his motive. Depend upon it, Dora, the reason is mixed up somehow with that dark story of the past."

"Well, well," said Dora with a sigh, "we shall know all when Mr. Carver comes. In the meantime, let us enjoy our present happiness."

Mrs. Tice approved of this sentiment, and brought in tea. The two lovers, with confidence restored between them, lingered over their simple meal, and made plans for the future. It was after six before they awoke to the fact that twilight was waning; and as Dora had to return to the Red House on her bicycle, Allen suggested that she should start at once. She demurred to this, as she was anxious to hear the lawyer's report of his interview with Joad, and while they were arguing the matter Mr. Carver arrived.

For so unemotional a man, he seemed greatly excited, and shook hands heartily with Dora, although he had seen her but a few hours before. Mr. Carver explained the meaning of that second salute.

"I congratulate you, young lady," he said heartily. "Through your cleverness and tact we have found out the truth. You are a heroine, Miss Carew."

"Not Miss Carew," interposed Allen brightly, "but Miss Dargill."

"I beg your pardon," said Mr. Carver in a stiff manner. "I am aware that Mr. Edermont's real name was Dargill, as you have no doubt learnt from the manuscript. But this young lady——"

"Is the daughter of your late client," interrupted Dora. "Captain Carew was not my father, Mr. Carver. I am the child of Julian Edermont—or rather, Dargill."

"In that case I congratulate you again, Miss Dora," said Carver, compromising the matter by calling her by her Christian name; "you can now marry Dr. Scott, since your father did not kill his father."

"Do you know that story?" asked Allen with a start.

"Oh dear, yes! I was told it by my late client. But he did not inform me that this young lady was his daughter. I was always under the impression that she was the child of Captain Carew, and the ward of the late Mr. Dargill. Strange he should have kept that from me," mused the lawyer; "but I never yet knew a client to tell the whole truth."

"But this is all very well," broke in Dora. "What has Joad done—fled to London?"

"No. He has been with me for the last two hours; and by this time"—Mr. Carver glanced at his watch—"he is no doubt back in his cottage."

"Back in his cottage?" echoed the doctor. "Did he not make a confession?"

"Certainly. It was written out and signed in my presence, with two witnesses—myself and one of my clerks—to testify to the signature."

"Then he confesses the murder?"

"Oh dear me, no!" said Carver dryly; "he does nothing of the sort; but he confesses as to who committed the murder."

"Didn't he do it himself?"

"No, Miss Dora, he did not. Our friend Joad is innocent; although," added the lawyer with an afterthought, "he may be described as an accessory after the fact."

"Then who killed my father?" cried Dora in blank amazement.

"Aha! that is a long, long story," replied Carver with a nod. "All in good time, my dear young lady. You tell me briefly what is contained in the manuscript, and I shall supply the sequel. Thus," added Mr. Carver, rubbing his dry hands, "we shall arrive at a clear and logical understanding of the whole complicated matter."

Both lovers protested against this proposal, but Carver firmly refused to speak a word until the gist of the manuscript was communicated to him. In the end they were reluctantly compelled to give way to the lawyer's obstinacy, and postpone the satisfaction of their own curiosity. Assisted by Allen, the young girl communicated all the details, but succeeded little in moving the emotions of Mr. Carver. Perhaps the sequel he referred to was more exciting than what they told him. But on this point the pair had a speedy opportunity of judging.

"It's a queer story," said Carver reflectively, "but I've heard queerer. It is the sequel that is the odd thing about this. Here is a man who for twenty years goes in dread of his life, and takes all manner of precautions to look after it. Yet, a few days after he has learnt that his enemy is dead and his life is safe, he is foully murdered. I am not a superstitious man, Miss Dora, but I see the finger of Fate in this. Your father was doomed to die a violent death, and his lifelong fears were justified by the result."

"But he was not killed by the man whom he expected to be his murderer."

"Quite true, Dr. Scott. He was killed by the man whom he did not expect to be his murderer."

"What do you mean?" cried Dora, rising. "Did my father know this man?"

"Intimately. He was the man who at one time saved Mr. Edermont from being caught by Captain Carew."

"You don't mean John Mallison?" shouted Allen in wide-eyed surprise. Mr. Carver nodded.

"That's the man. He killed Edermont. You must admit that there is something ironical in the fact?"

"I don't understand it at all," said Dora helplessly. "Will you be so kind as to tell us how and why the crime was committed?"

"Willingly," replied Carver, and commenced forthwith. "My late client, as you know, went for years in fear of his life," he said in his dry way; "but shortly before the murder his fears were ended by a communication from a Mr. Pallant. This gentleman told him that Captain Carew had died in San Francisco, and as a reward for his intelligence asked Mr. Edermont for a packet of letters written by Lady Burville to her second husband. Mr. Edermont was unwilling to give them up, as he saw that Pallant wanted to blackmail the unfortunate woman—your mother, Miss Dora. He refused to comply with Mr. Pallant's request, and wrote to Lady Burville at Hernwood Hall, asking her to come to his study in the Red House on the night of the second of August between eleven and twelve o'clock, when he undertook to give her up the letters."

"But why did he choose so late an hour?"

"Because he did not wish to compromise Lady Burville's

position; nor did he wish Pallant to know. This letter he posted himself. But Joad—who was afraid of losing his home with his patron, and thinking something was wrong—obtained the letter in some way from the village post-office, and made himself master of its contents. Those he communicated to me as I have told them. So you see," continued Mr. Carter, "that Edermont expected a visit from Lady Burville on that night. He also expected a visit from Scott."

"Yes," said Allen eagerly; "he wrote to me, and appointed almost the same hour. But why?"

"I will tell you, doctor. He wished to give Lady Burville the letters, but only conditionally that in your presence she admitted that Dora was her child."

"Oh! so he repented telling me that Carew killed my father?"

"No; but he repented letting you remain under the impression that Dora was the child of your father's murderer. That, as he knew, was a bar to your marriage, and to do away with it he asked you to meet Lady Burville."

"But I did not meet her!"

"No; because you were late, and she would not wait. But let us continue. Edermont also wrote a letter to Mallison, telling him that now Carew was dead, and his fears at an end, he would no longer pay him the pension he had hitherto allowed him. That letter was the cause of his death."

"But how?" asked Dora and Allen together.

"You shall hear. Joad, learning, as I have said, about the appointment with Lady Burville, made up his mind to overhear the conversation. He knew by the letter he had opened that the postern-gate and the glass-door were to be left ajar, so about eleven o'clock he got into the house that way."

"Without being seen by Mr. Edermont?"

"Yes. Mr. Edermont at that moment was in his bedroom, so Joad slipped through the study and hid in the darkness of the hall. Here he altered the clock by putting it on an hour."

"But why did he do that?"

"In case Edermont should suspect him the next day," explained Carver; "then he could prove an alibi by saying he was in his cottage. He did this with success to clear himself of the murder, but primarily it was to make himself safe in the eyes of Edermont."

"Well, we know that he altered the clock. What happened then?"

"Lady Burville arrived, and Edermont, returning to the study, gave her the letters. Joad, hidden behind the door, saw and heard all. Edermont showed her the manuscript, which he took out of the bureau, and told her he was going to burn it and alter his will. Afterwards, when Dr. Scott did not come, she refused to wait, and went off. Edermont saw her to the glass-door at the end of the deserted drawing-room. He left the manuscript on the desk; and, seeing a way to get a hold over Edermont, Joad stepped into the room during his absence and secured it."

"The scoundrel!" cried Dora excitedly. "Go on, Mr. Carver."

"Hardly had Joad hidden himself again when Edermont came back in a state of terror, with Mallison at his heels. Mallison reproached him for cutting off his income, and swore he would obtain the manuscript, which he knew was in the bureau, and reveal the whole story. He began to pull out the drawers, smash the desk, and toss the papers all out. Edermont raved and implored and threatened. Ultimately he took out a pistol to shoot Mallison, in the extremity of his terror. Mallison, to defend himself, caught the knobkerrie from the wall. The first barrel of the revolver proved empty, and before Edermont could fire again, Mallison killed him by smashing in his head with the club."

"Horrible! And Joad?"

"When he saw the murder he rushed in, and tried to raise an alarm. Mallison caught him by the throat, and swore he would kill him also if he did not hold his tongue. Joad, in terror, promised to do so. Then the clock struck one. Mallison looked at his watch and found it was only twelve. Seeing a chance of proving an alibi for them both, he dragged Joad out of the house into his cottage; and so he was safe. It was shortly after they entered the cottage that Dr. Scott came down the road. He entered, saw the evidence of the crime, and fled."

"And why did Joad hold his tongue?"

"Because Mallison found out he had the manuscript, which Joad hid and would not give up. He swore he would say that Joad had committed the crime if he did not keep quiet. You can see for yourself the position in which Joad was placed. Of two evils he chose the least, and held his peace. But when he found that the manuscript was gone, he thought Mallison had taken it, and, fearful for his life lest Mallison should denounce him to gain the fifty thousand pounds, he came in to-day and confided all to me."

"I understand all," said Dora—"all but one point. Who is John Mallison?"

"Why," said Carver quietly, "none other than your polite friend, Mr. Pride."

CHAPTER XXVI

A FINAL SURPRISE

And now that the mysterious criminal has been discovered, nothing remains but to relate the end of some and the future of others—meaning all those persons who, directly or indirectly, have been connected in any way with the tragic death of Julian Edermont.

In the first place, Joad died of heart disease. This organ had been affected for some considerable period, and he had always been told to live quietly and to avoid excitement. For years he had taken this advice, and had vegetated at the Red House; but the dread of what Mallison might do to him, and the excitement of the subsequent arrest, proved too much for him. He fell dead on his own doorstep on the very night on which the murderer was arrested.

"Although," said the Morning Planet, commenting on this event, "it was perhaps as well that he did not live. He might have been arrested for keeping silence as to his knowledge of the assassin. He was an accessory after the fact, and in his terror he compounded a felony; so, probably, if he had lived the law would have taken cognisance of his behaviour. But as it was, Lambert Joad died worth fifty thousand pounds. By the will of Julian Edermont, this amount was left to the person who should bring his murderer to justice. Mr. Joad did this, as it was through his instrumentality that the criminal Mallison, alias Pride, was secured by the police. He was arrested in Joad's cottage, whither in the evening he had gone to see the old man, and owing to the excitement of the struggle and subsequent capture, Joad fell dead of heart disease. His gaining of the reward did him but little good. But it will now go to his relatives, if he has any, and should prove a lucky windfall for them."

Although Lady Burville's name was kept out of the papers, a rumour got about that she was connected in some way with the case. Nothing very definite was known as to how she was implicated, but it was hinted that in some vague way the death was due to her influence. Alarmed at this hint of publicity, and tired of being blackmailed by Pallant, the little woman plucked up her small portion of courage, and confessed the whole story to Sir John. Needless to say, the millionaire was deeply shocked, but as he recognised that his wife was one of those weak fools of women who bring trouble on themselves and on everyone else, he forgave her. He trusted to the influence of his strong nature to keep her in the right path for the future, and, indeed, as Laura Burville had an assured position—for Sir John insisted upon marrying her again after he knew that Carew was really dead—and plenty of money, she had no temptation to behave badly. After the confession and second marriage and forgiveness, she felt much happier than she had done since the tragedy at Christchurch. Her fate was a better one than she had a right to expect.

With Pallant, who knew that Lady Burville had not been actually married, seeing that Carew still lived, when the first ceremony took place, Sir John came to a compromise. He paid him a handsome sum of money, for which he received a receipt. Then he turned the blackmailer out of the house, made him leave England, and swore if he ever set foot in London again that he would prosecute him for blackmailing. As Pallant knew that Sir John was a man of his word, and, moreover, as he had reaped a rich harvest by his blackguardly conduct, he willingly went abroad. Ultimately he returned to San Francisco, and was shot in a Chinese gambling shop while playing fan-tan. No one regretted him when he died, and the only people who gave him a thought were the Burvilles, who breathed more freely when they saw an account of the tragedy. So Augustus Pallant was punished in the long-run for his many villainies.

And the still greater villain, John Mallison, came to his right end also. He refused to admit his guilt, but, thanks to the evidence of Meg Gance, who deposed as to the alteration of the clock, and to the confession of Joad, he was arrested, and tried for the murder of his quondam friend. The jury brought him in guilty, and he was condemned to death. At the last moment he confessed that the charge was true.

"I did kill Julian Dargill," he confessed, the night before his execution, "and I am glad that I rid the world of the crawling little ingrate. Twenty and more years ago I saved his life from the bullet of Carew at the risk of my own. I took his name, and led Carew off to America on a false trail; and had it not been for the dexterity with which I avoided him, I should have been killed by my pursuer in mistake for Dargill. And for this service Julian allowed me only a paltry two hundred a year. I turned tutor and took the name of Pride at Chillum to keep Dargill under my eye; and I had to have some excuse for remaining in so dull a hole.

"Julian was afraid to tell me face to face that he intended to cut off my pension. The coward wrote, although I was at Chillum at the time. It was no coincidence that I was in the study between the visits of Lady Burville and Scott. I learnt from Joad, who opened the letter to Lady Burville, that Edermont expected those two at midnight on the second of August. I wanted to go and taunt him before them with his mean conduct. I did not intend to kill him, but only to taunt him, and to get possession of the manuscript, so as to force him to continue my pension. But he threatened me with a pistol, and in self-defence I killed him. The blow was unpremeditated, but, since it killed him, I refuse to say that I am sorry. I knew that Joad had secured the manuscript, but he refused to give it up, and I could not find out where he had hidden it. If I had secured the manuscript, no one would have known that John Mallison was in existence, and I would then have denounced Joad as the assassin and gained the fifty thousand pounds. It was his belief that I had taken it instead of Miss Dora that made him tell Carver the truth. But he is dead, too, the miserable traitor! I shall have one satisfaction in going to the scaffold in knowing that the man who injured me and the man who betrayed me have gone before. Both their deaths, directly and indirectly, can be laid at my door. I'm glad of it."

As to Dora, there was some difficulty over her marriage—this time through her own scruples about her birth. She reminded Allen of the blot upon her life—that she had not even a right to the name of Dargill, much less that of Carew. But Allen laughed away her scruples and kissed away her tears, and swore that she should be his wife in the spring. Dora yielded to his persuasions and to those of Mrs. Tice, and surrendered herself to the full tide of happiness which was bearing her along to a prosperous future. So all was settled, and then came a final surprise from no less a person than Mr. Carver.

Shortly after Mallison, alias Pride, had paid the penalty of his crime, the lovers were seated on the lawn of the Red House, under the shadow of the mighty cedar. It was a quiet and beautiful evening, just after sunset, and the sky was resplendent with colours like the hues of a butterfly's wing. Allen's arm was round the waist of Dora, and they were talking of their future.

"I think it will be best for you to come to Canterbury, Dora," he was saying. "After the tragedy which has taken place in this house, you can never live in it without a shudder. Marry me, live in Canterbury, and we will keep on Mrs. Tice as housekeeper."

"But I lose what little fortune I have if I leave it," remonstrated the girl.

"What of that? I can give you a comfortable home, dearest. My practice is increasing, and in a few years we shall be quite opulent. Give up your father's bequest, my own, and let us begin our new life without dwelling within the shadow of a crime."

While Dora was reflecting what answer to make, the gate opened—it was never locked now—and Mr. Carver, as black as a raven and as lean as a stick, made his appearance. He saw the couple on the lawn, and walked directly towards them, with what was meant for a smile on his grim face. Indeed, he had taken a great fancy to the young couple—to Dora in particular—and they both welcomed him heartily.

"Well, my young friends," said he, when the first greetings were over, "I have come to learn your plans."

"We were just making them," said Dora with a blush. "Allen wants me to give up the Red House and live in Canterbury when we are married."

"I agree with him there, Miss Dora. The Red House is what the Scotch call uncanny. I should not like to live in it myself, with the knowledge that a brutal murder had been committed within its walls."

"I feel the same as you do," replied Dora. "All the same, if I give it up I lose my poor two hundred a year, and shall go to Allen a pauper."

"Dearest, as if that mattered! I can provide a home for you, and Mrs. Tice shall look after it."

"Be comforted, Miss Dora," said Carver, smiling. "You will not go to Allen a pauper. You are entitled to fifty thousand pounds—your father's money."

"But why, Mr. Carver? I did not find out who killed my father."

"No; but Joad did, and the money came to him. On the day that he made his confession—as if anticipating his untimely end—he made his will, and left all the money to you."

"All the money to Dora?" cried Allen joyfully. "Then she inherits her father's money, after all!"

"Every penny of it," replied Carver gravely; "and I'm glad to say so."

"But—but can I take it?" said Dora in a hesitating manner.

"Tut, tut! Why not? You need have no compunction in doing so, my dear. As your father's daughter and sole offspring, he should have left it to you. It has only passed through Joad's hands on its way to your pockets. Take it by all means. I kept the telling of this for you as a pleasant surprise. Do not spoil my little plot by a refusal."

"What do you say, Allen?"

"I say with Mr. Carver, my dear, take it—it is lawfully yours."

"Then I shall accept it. Fifty thousand pounds! O Allen!" Dora flung her arms round his neck. "You can go to London—we can take a house in Harley Street—you can become a famous physician—and—and——"

"And all your geese will be swans!" laughed Carver kindly.

But Allen did not laugh. He held Dora to his breast and kissed her.

"My dearest," he said in a grave tone, "the money is not unwelcome; but a greater gift has come to me than that—the gift of a true-hearted, stanch woman, who will be a noble wife."

"Hear, hear!" said Carver the misogamist. And so that disturbed chapter in their lives came to an end.

THE END

Milton Keynes UK
Ingram Content Group UK Ltd.
UKHW040715201124
451458UK00015B/109/J

9 798889 424789